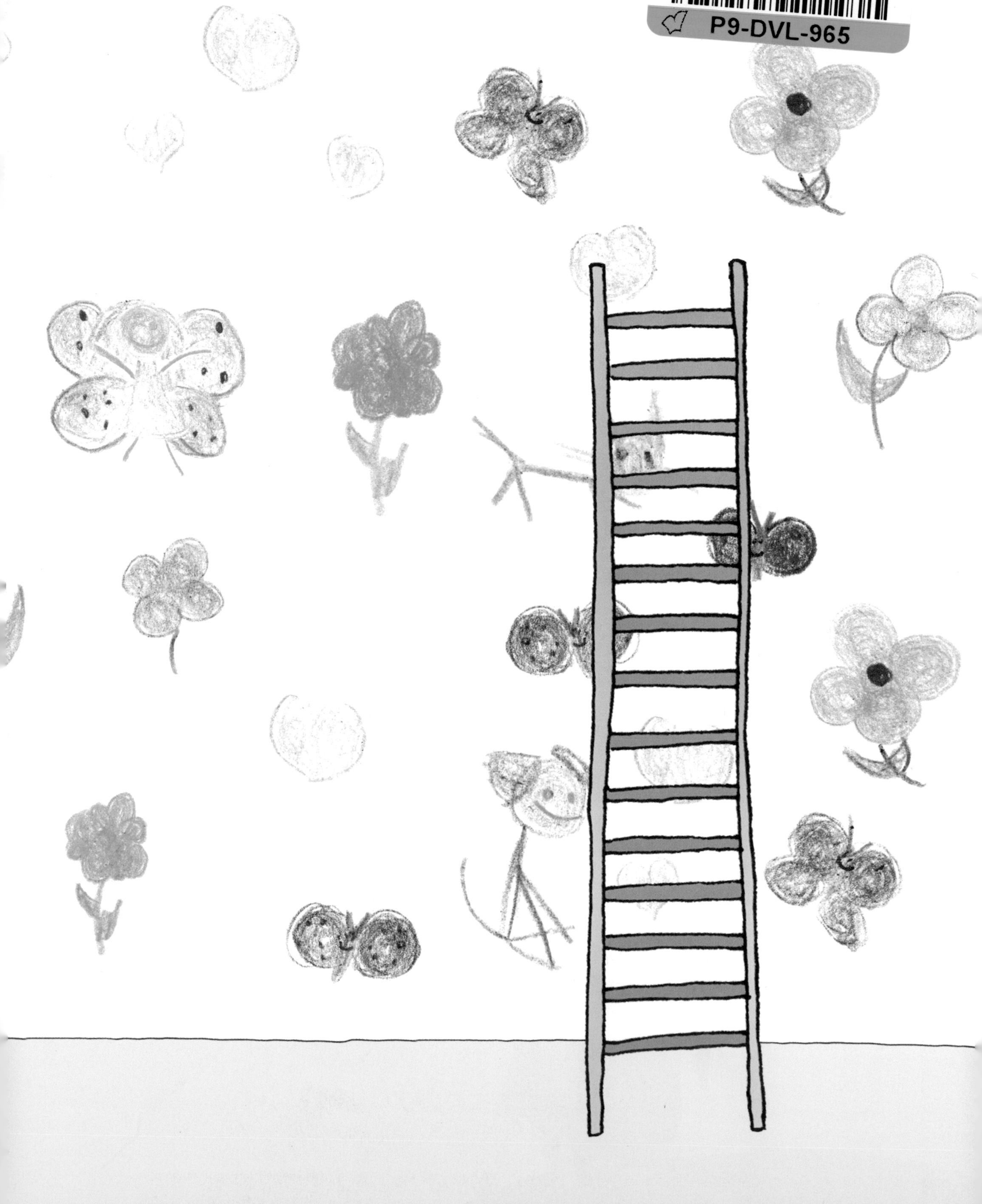

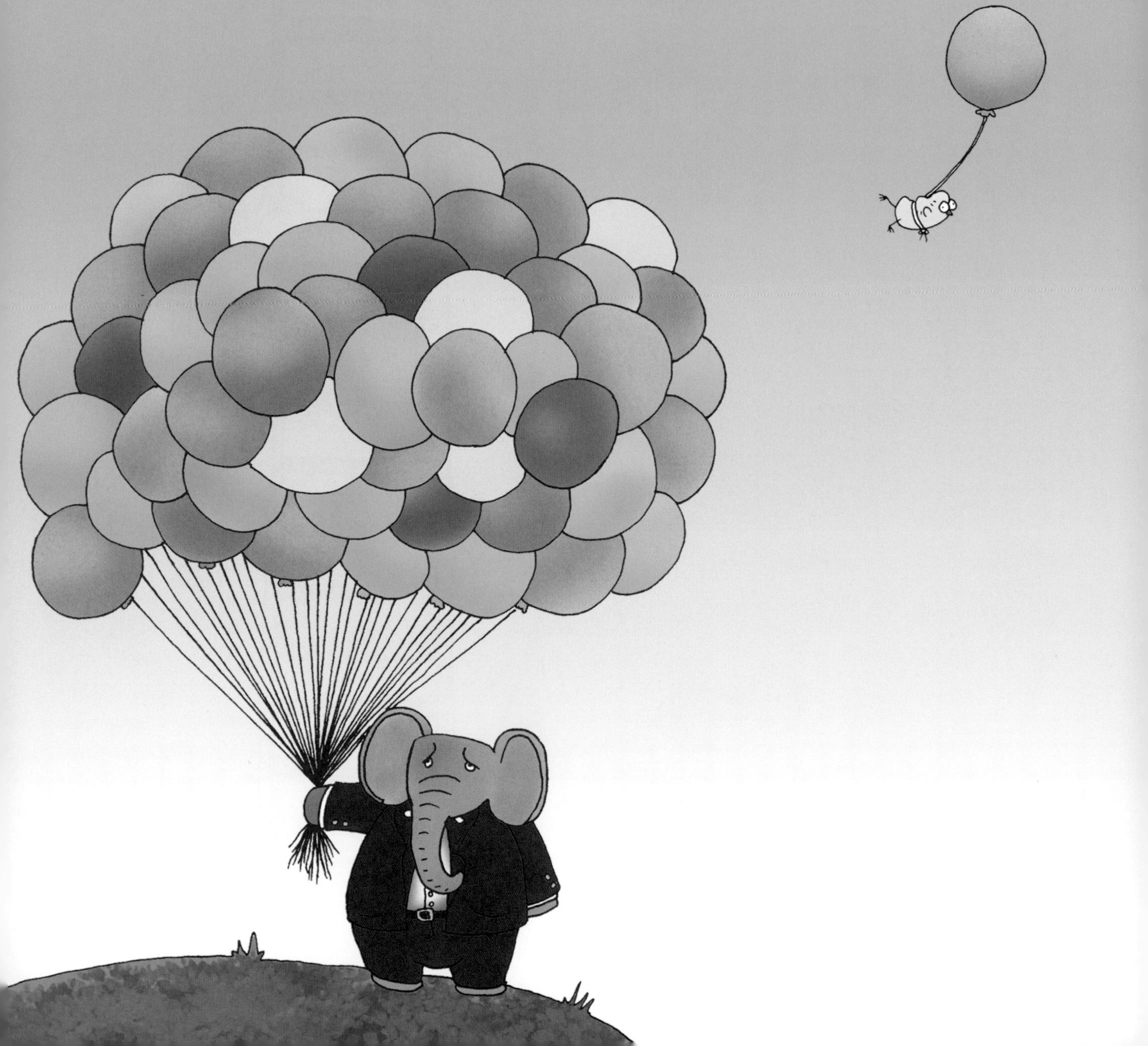

This book is given with love

_____

_____

Published in the United States
by Puppy Dogs & Ice Cream, Inc.
ISBN: 978-1-953177-14-8
Edition: July 2020

For all inquiries, please contact us at:
info@puppysmiles.org

To see more of our books, visit us at:
www.PuppyDogsAndIceCream.com

Created by April & Jackson Jones

REVERIE

I believe in me

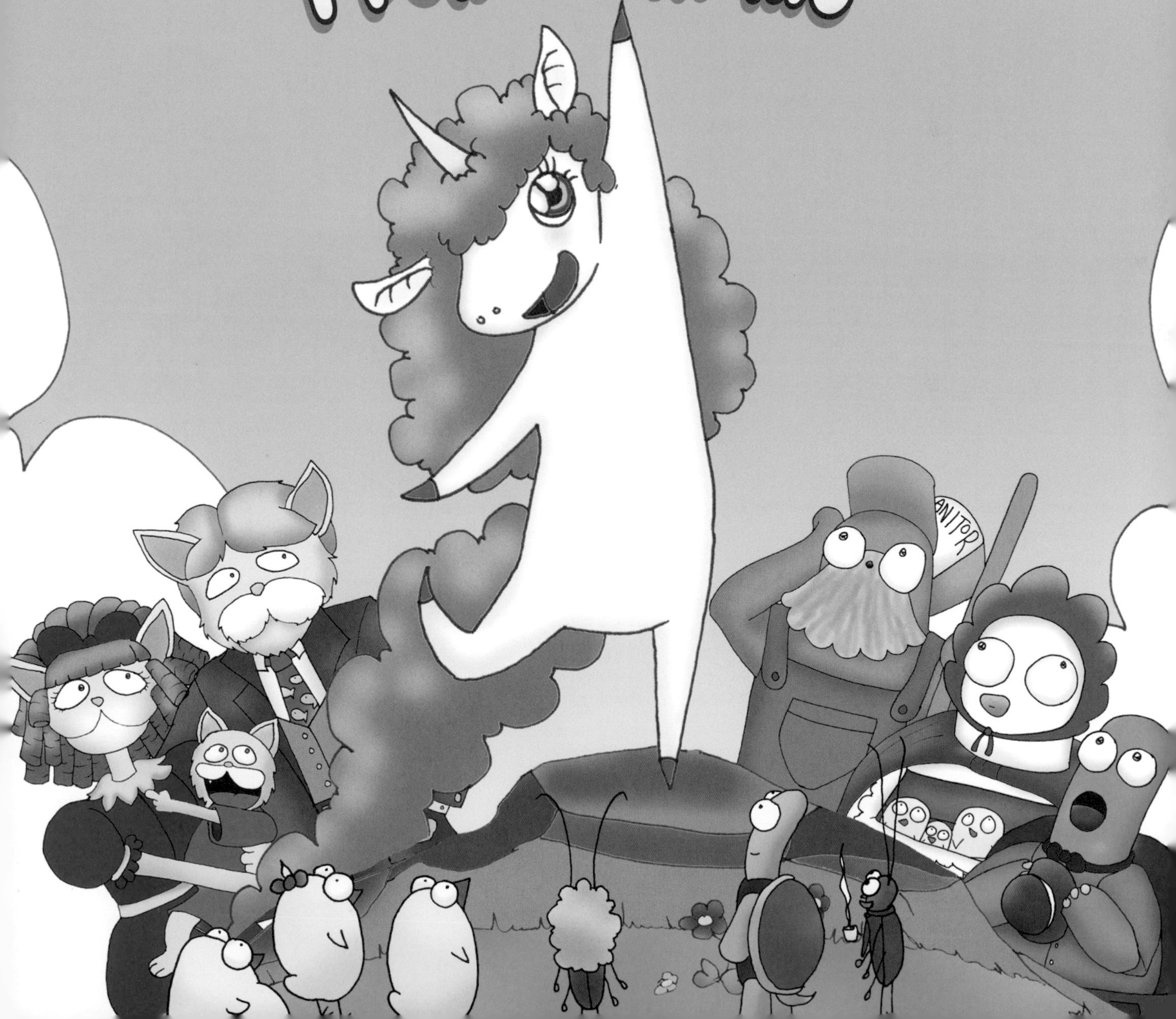

Reverie was a small unicorn,
Her mane and coat were so fair...
She had big dreams to fulfill,
As for how, she did not care.

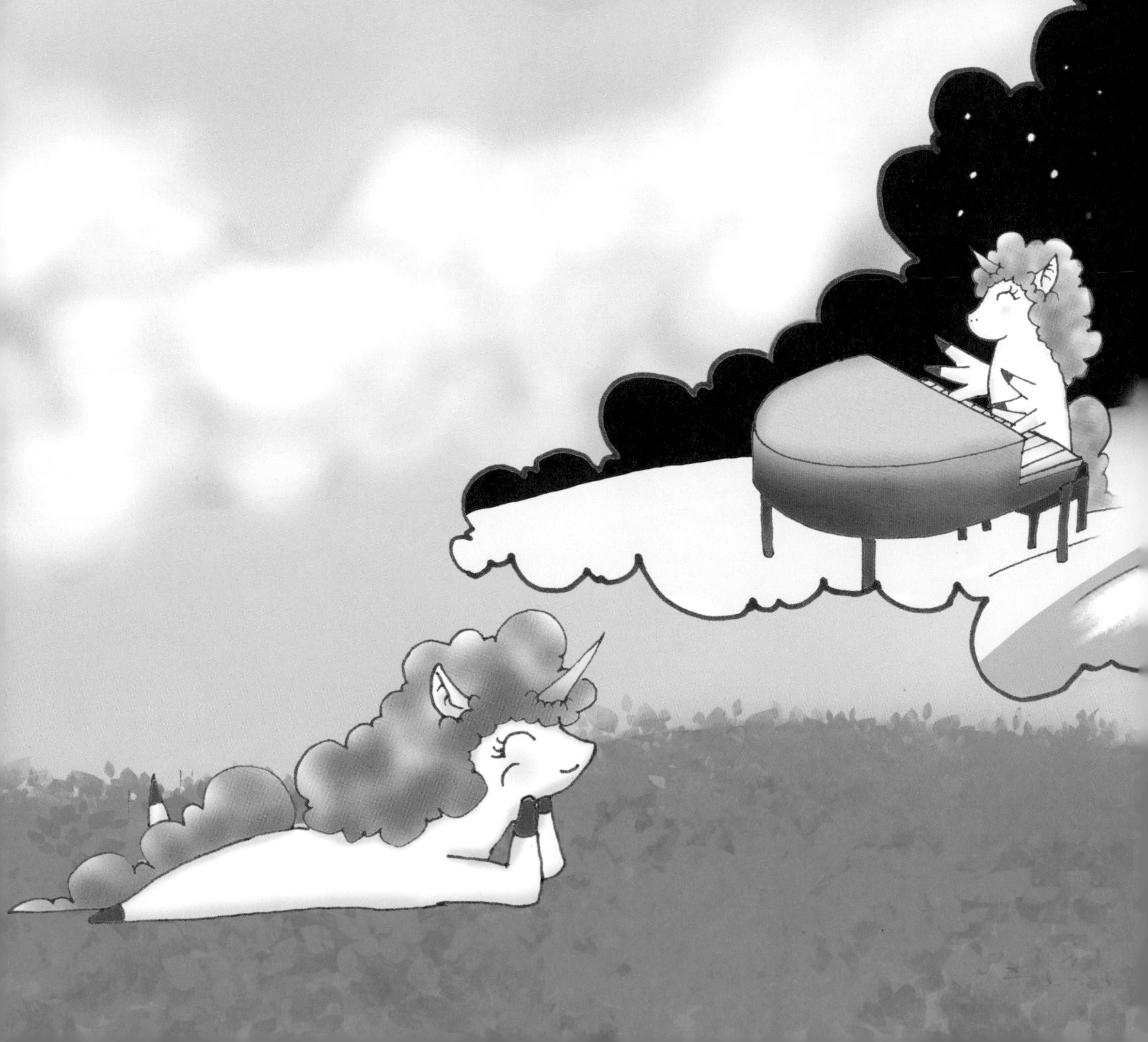

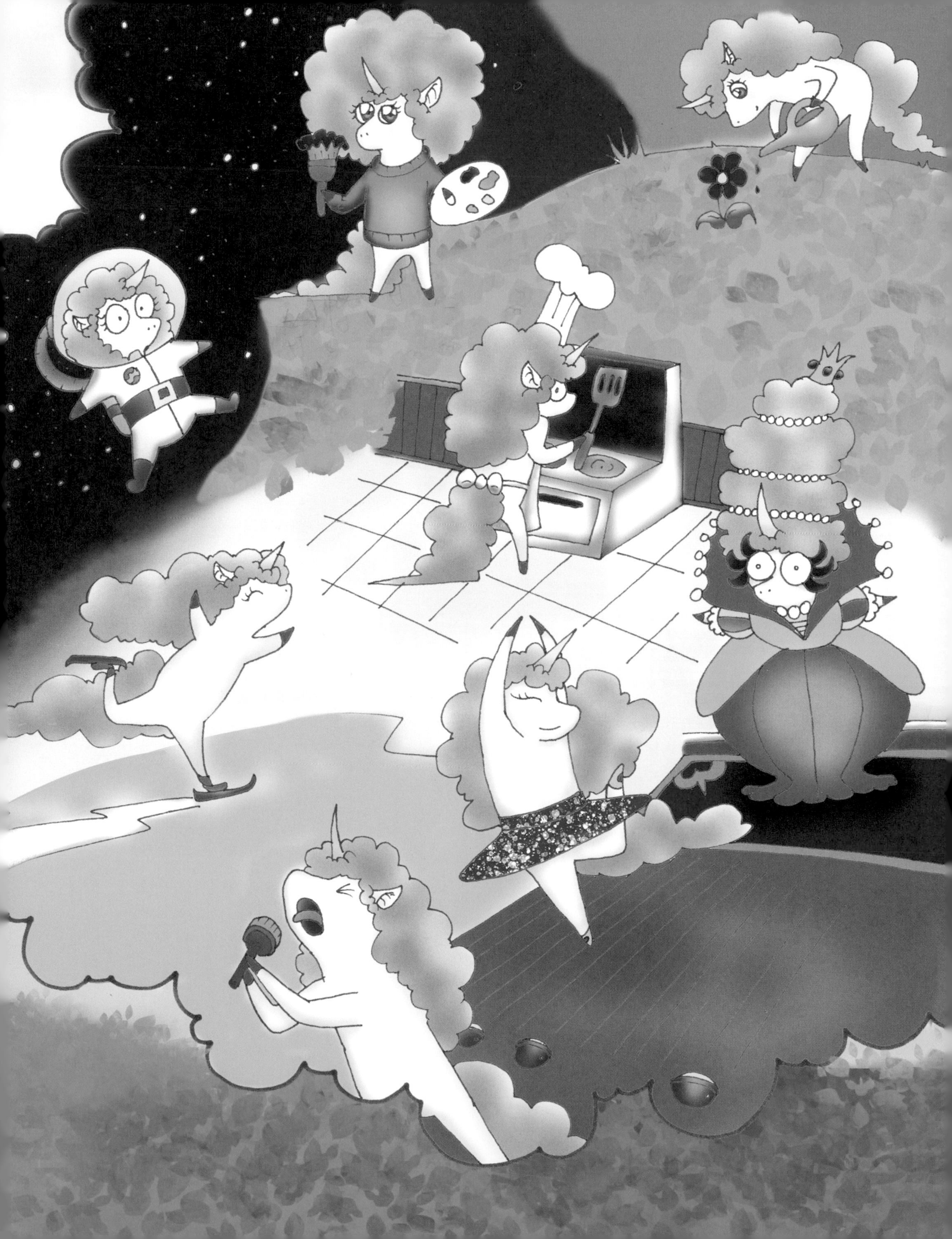

Her little hooves worked really hard,
Baking up a storm...
She set up shop, threw sprinkles on,
Her pastries still all warm.

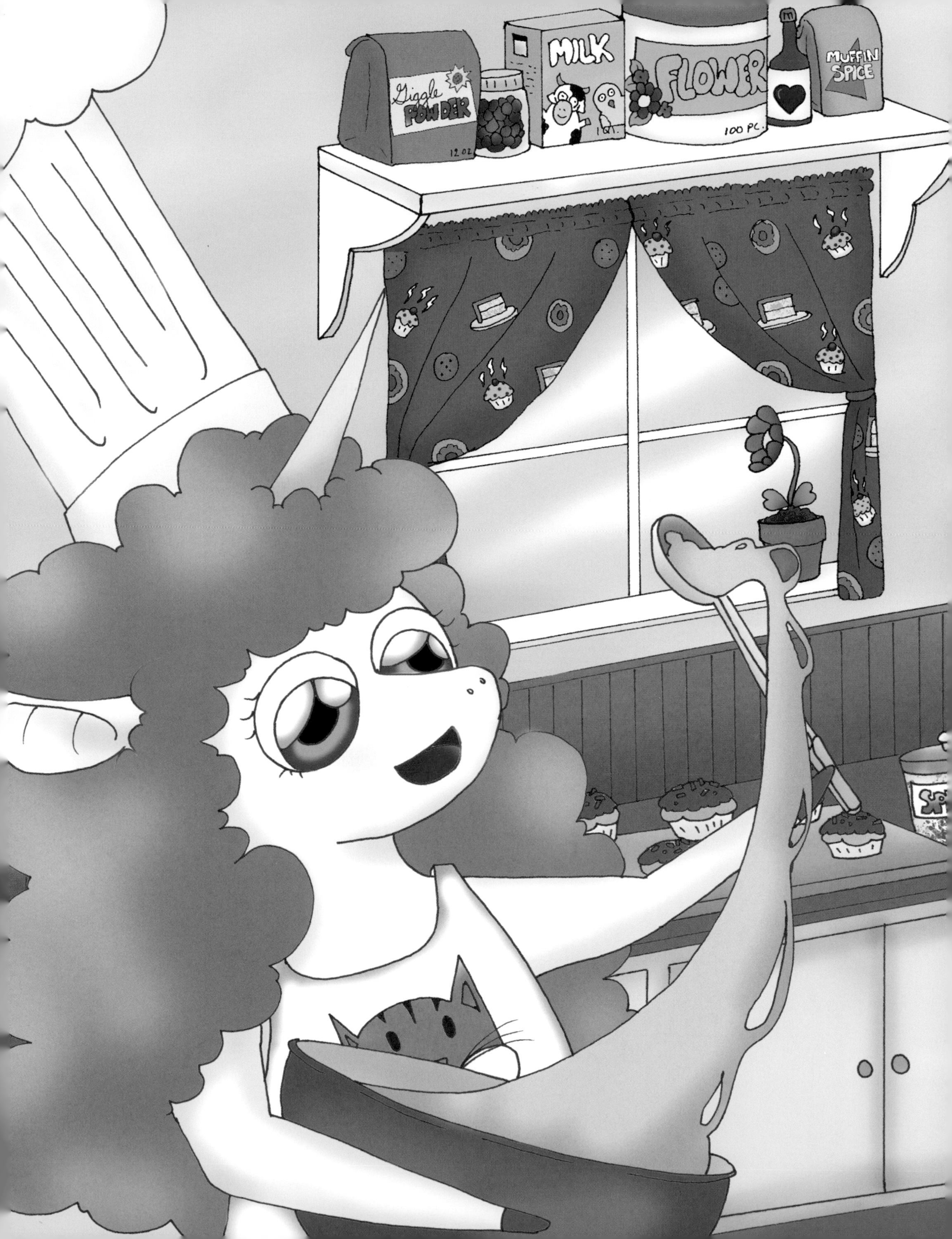
Giggle
POWDER
12 OZ.
MILK
1 QT.
FLOWER
100 PC.
MUFFIN
SPICE

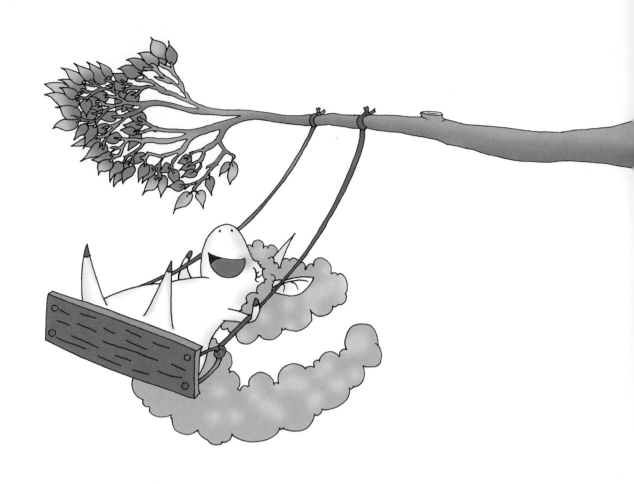

Dubiety the Fox walked up,
And noticed all her glee...
"What's all this?" he asked perplexed,
"It's just too much for me."

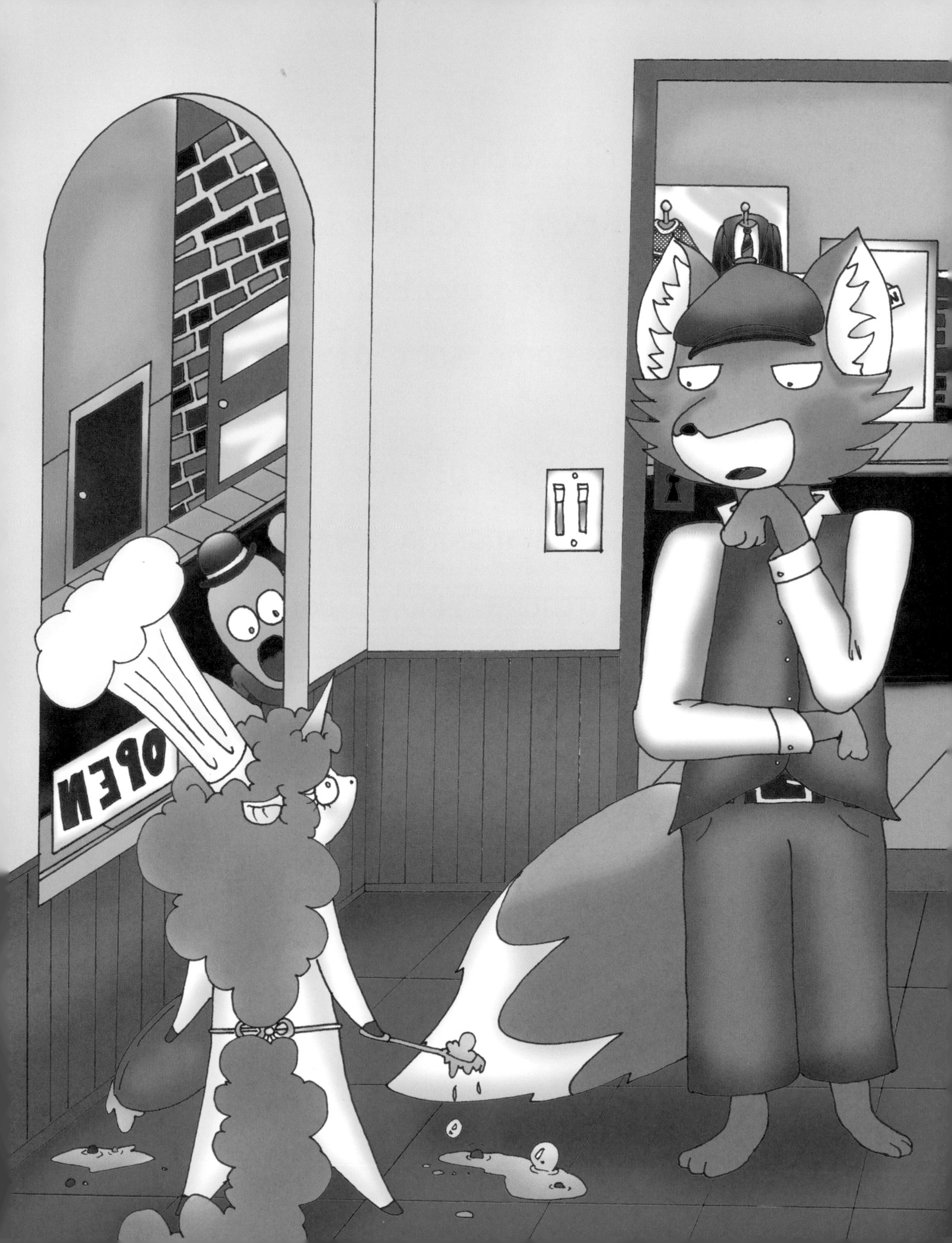
OPEN

"I'm setting up my bakery shop,"
Reverie exclaimed...
"A Unicorn?!" the Fox inquired,
"Is this some sort of game?"

"Whoever heard of such a thing,
Unicorns making sweets!"
"There's many others who've done the same,
And they all have you beat."

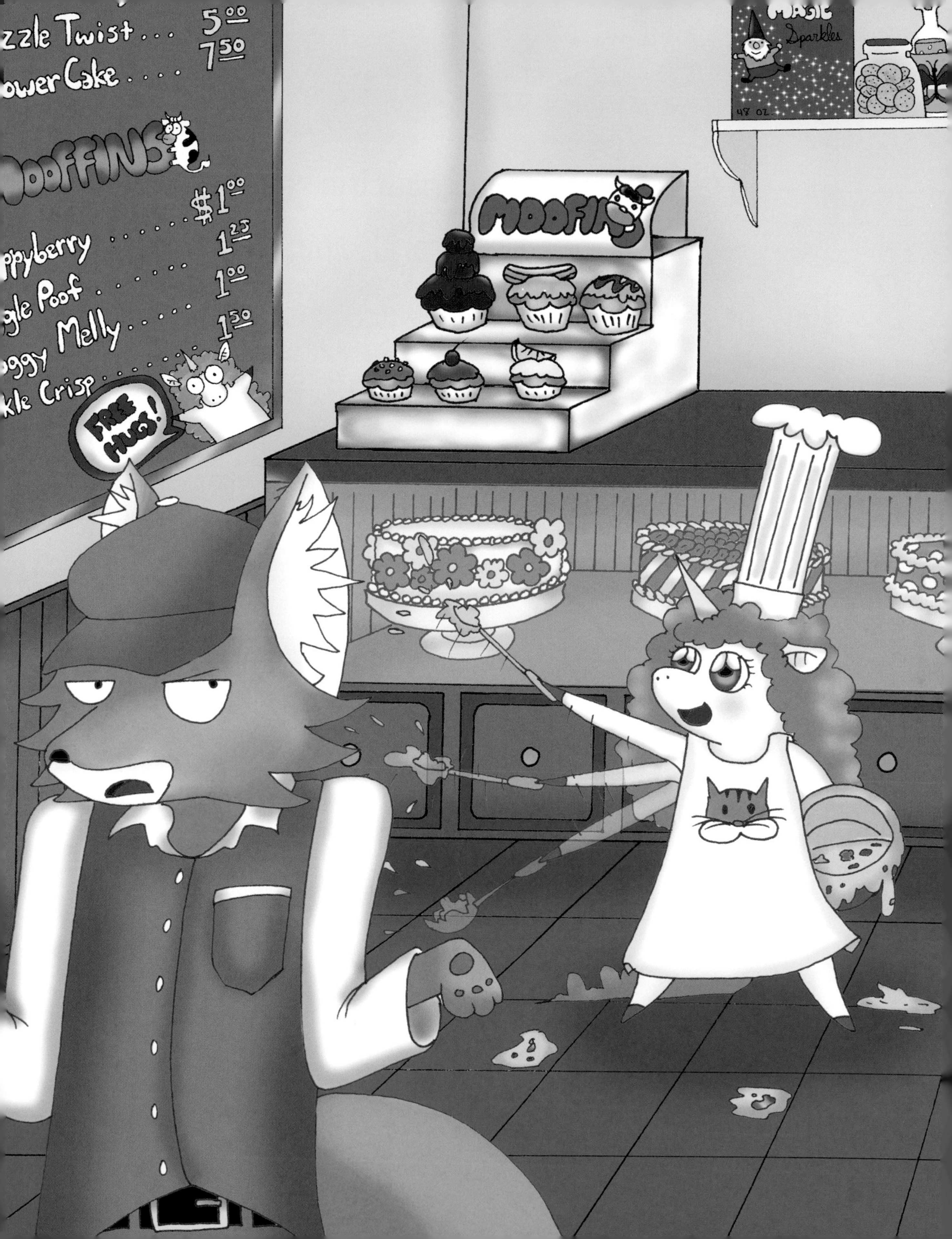

zzle Twist ... 5.00
ower Cake 7.50
ooFFINS
$1.00
ppyberry 1.25
gle Poof 1.00
ggy Melly 1.50
kle Crisp
FREE HUGS!
MOOFI
MAGIC
Sparkles
48 OZ.

Reverie, once hearing this,
Began to sit and think...
Her heart and dreams were much too big,
For her to let them sink.

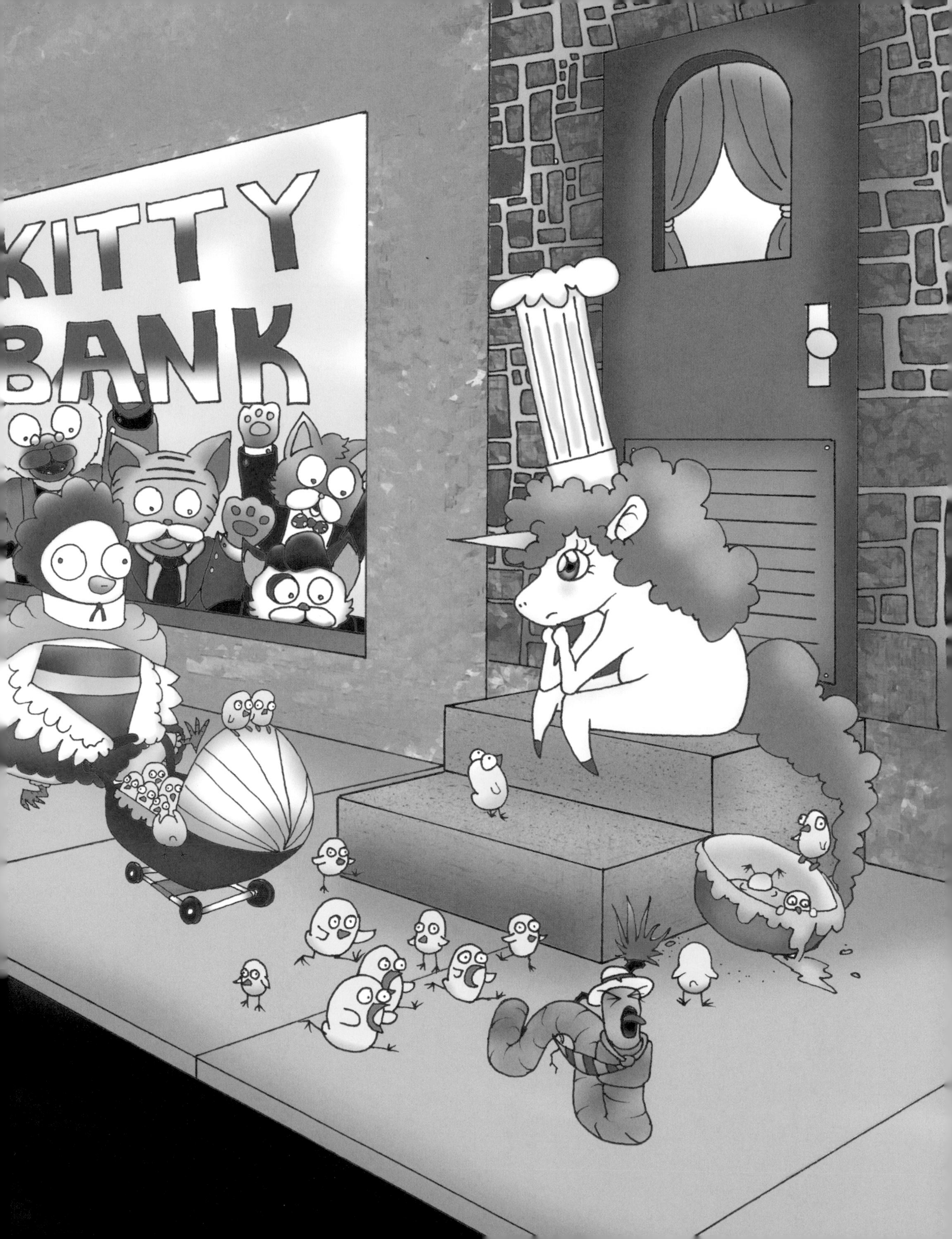
KITTY
BANK

"There are so many other things
That I still have yet to try..."
Saying this, she set to work,
With hair coloring and dye.

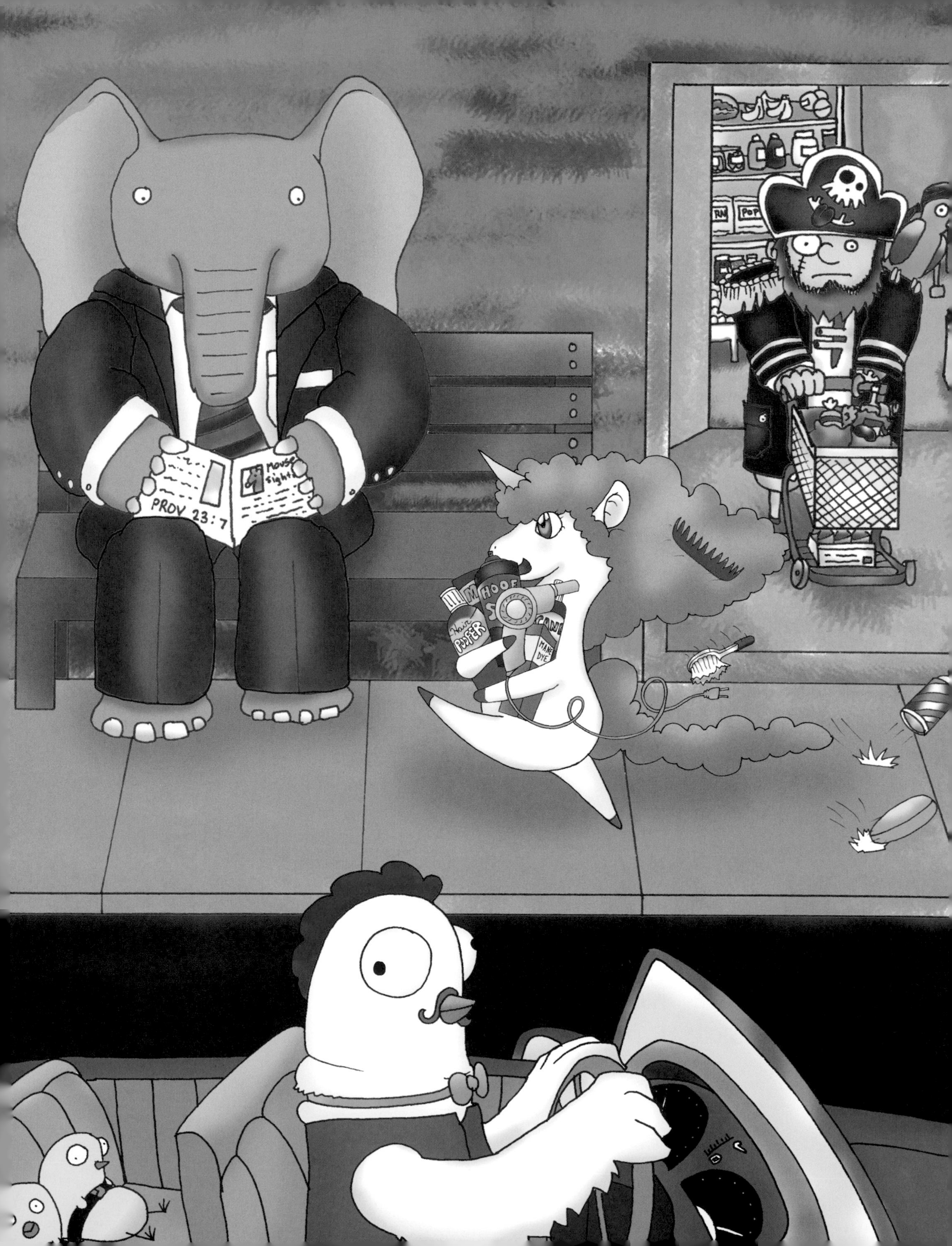
PROV 23:7
Hair POOFER
HOOF
MANE DYE

Her little hooves worked their magic,
With hair she would poof and preen...
When Jealousy the Bird flew in,
Eyes narrowed at the scene.

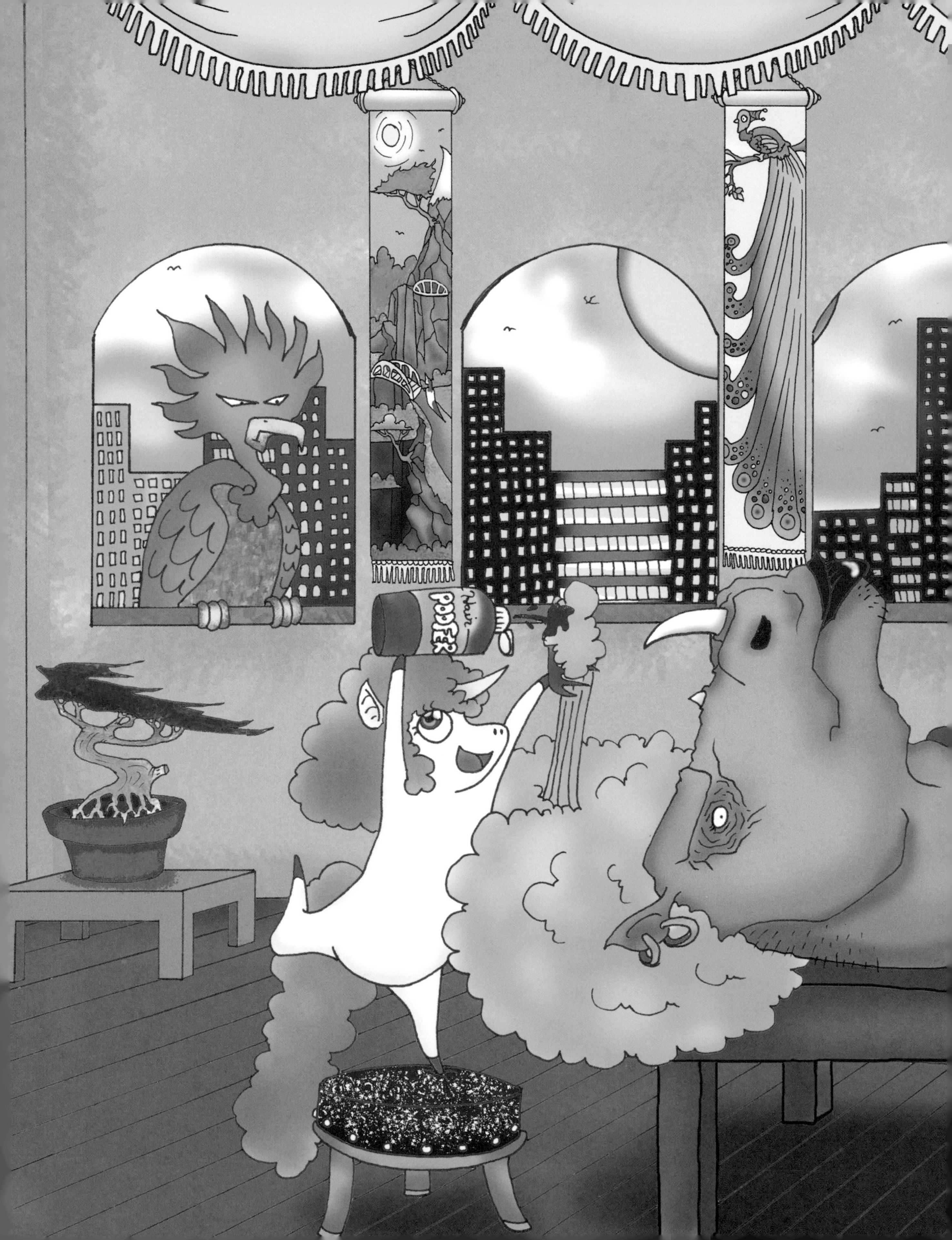
Hair
POOFER

"What's this?!" Jealousy squawked in ire,
You could tell she was not pleased...
"It's my salon," Reverie replied,
Looking quite uneased.

"A Salon?" scoffed Jealousy,
In utter disbelief...
"Give up this foolish flight of fancy,
It will only cause you grief."

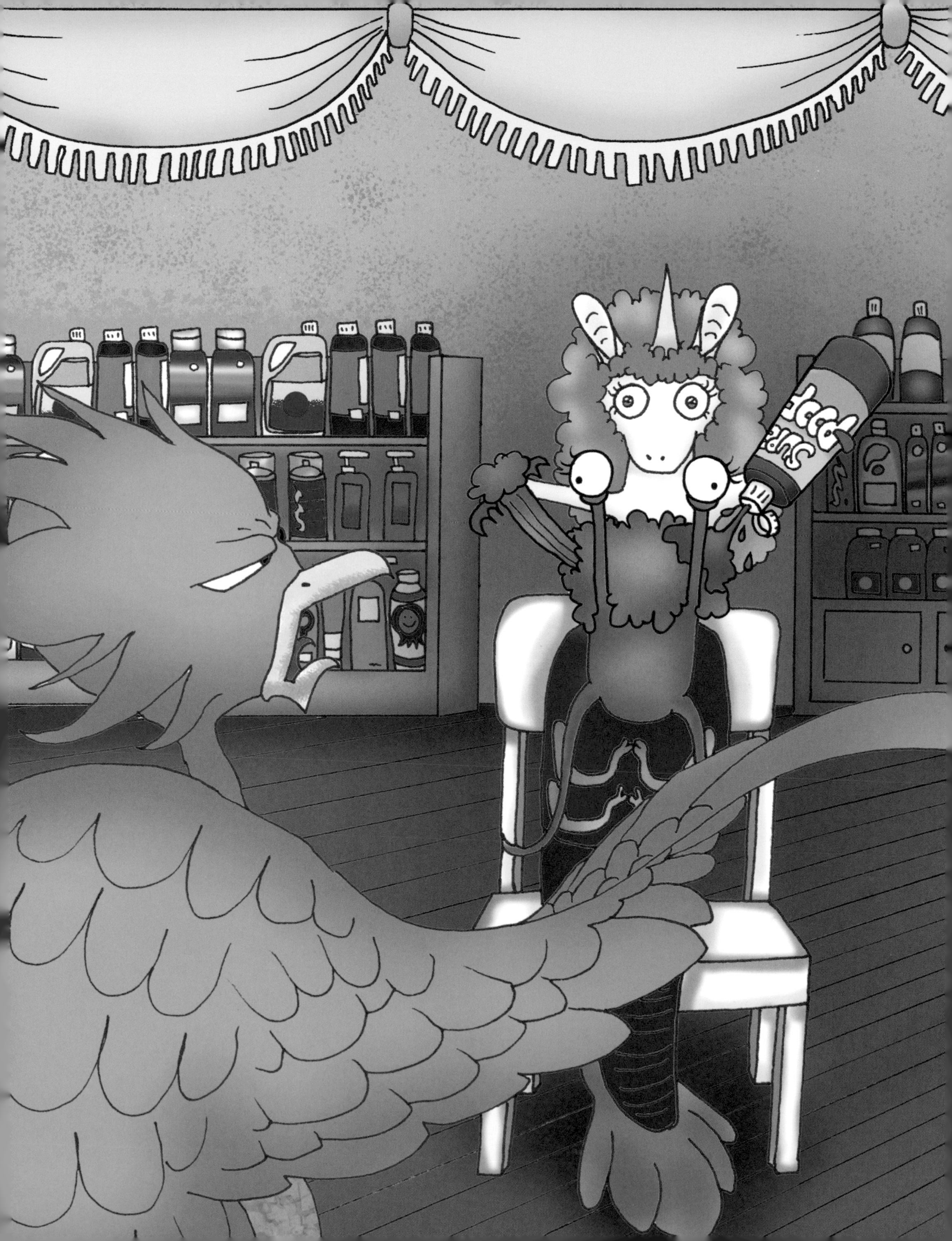
SUP
GOOP

Reverie thought freshly,
Of more talents she possessed...
For, with creativity,
She was greatly blessed.

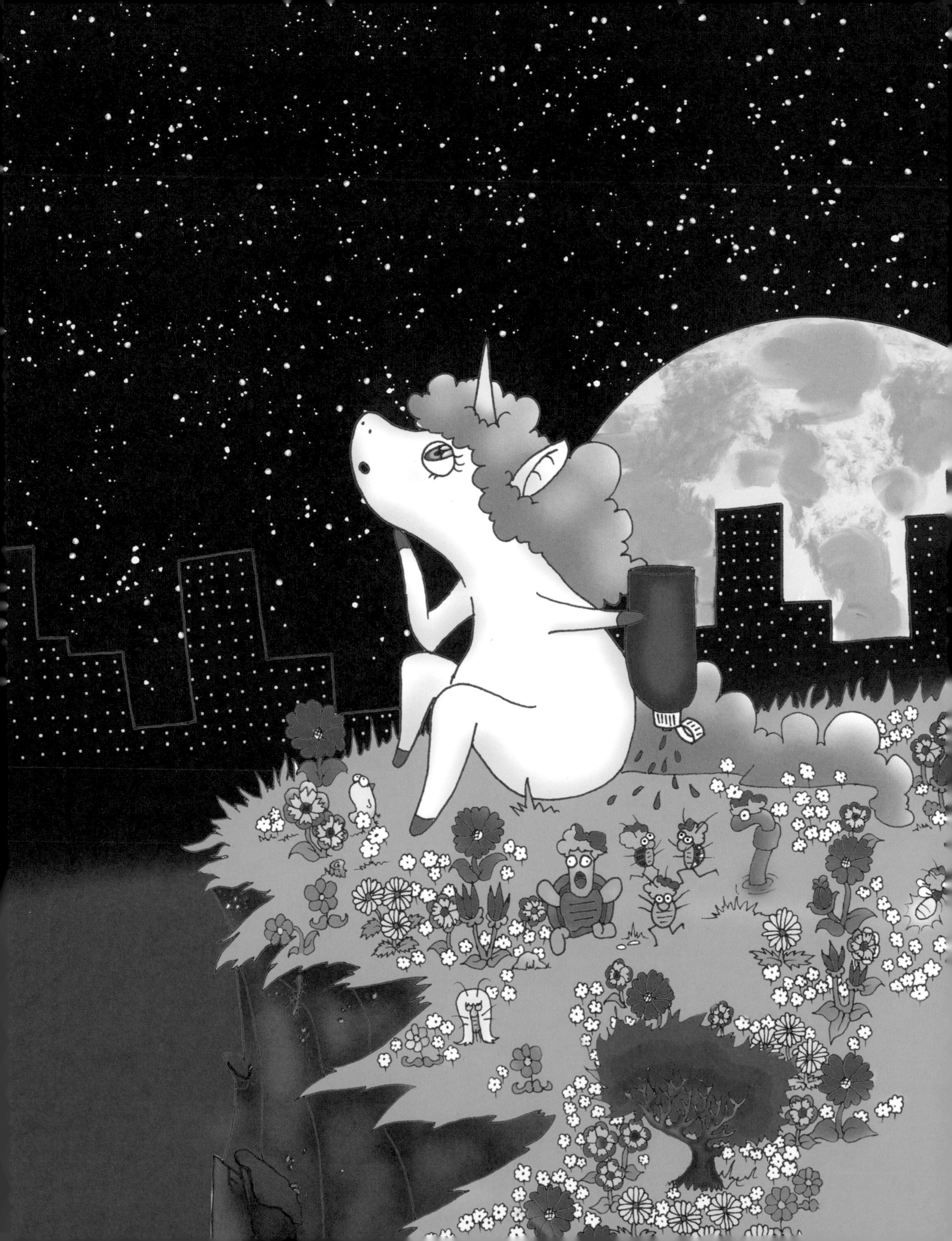

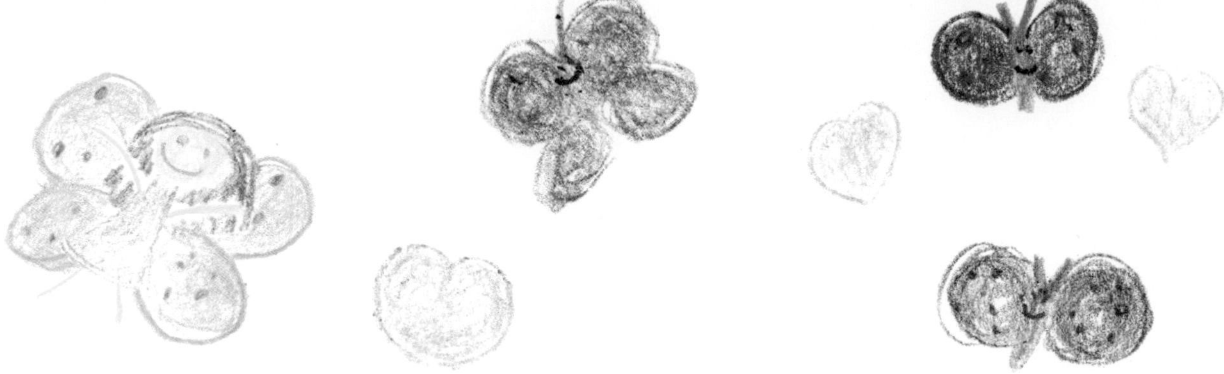

A dance studio, Reverie thought,
Her new idea seemed sound...
Twirling in her sparkly tutu
With every single bound.

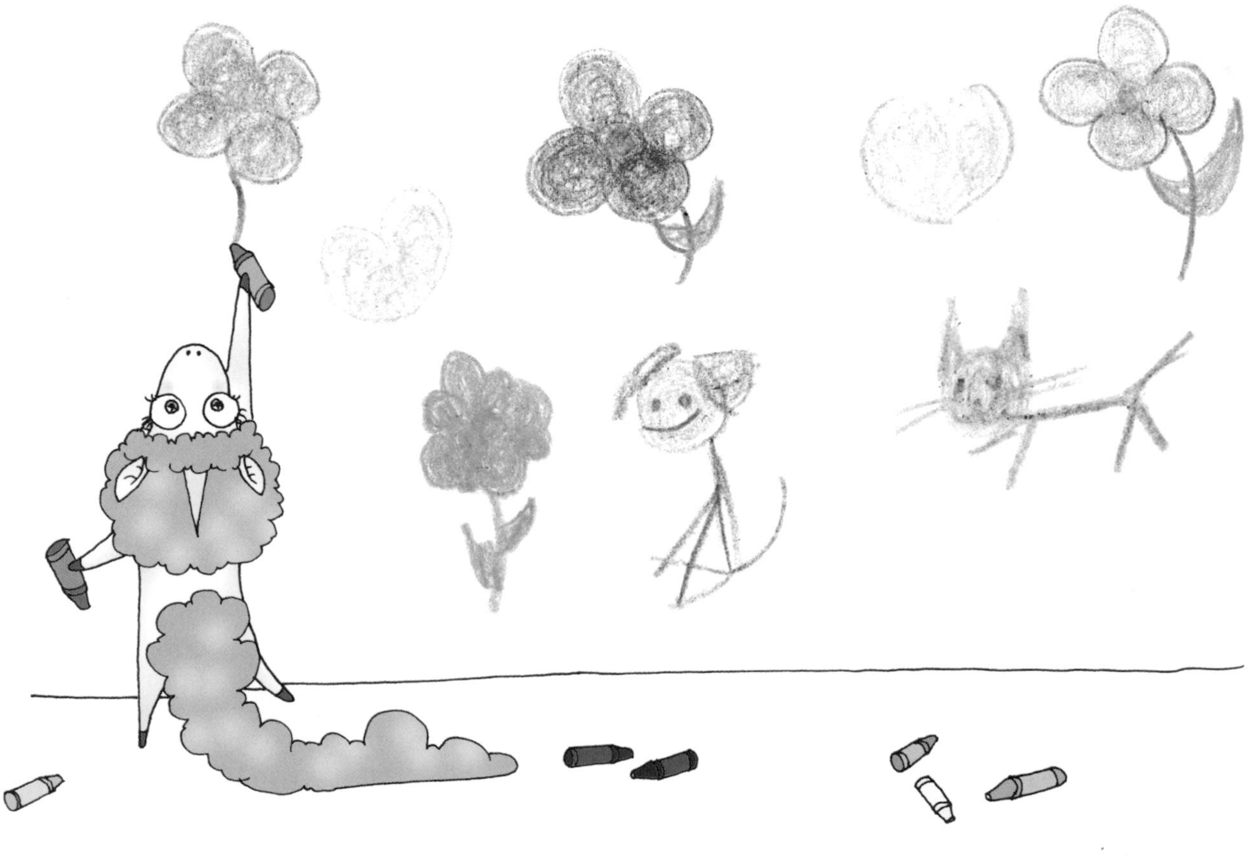

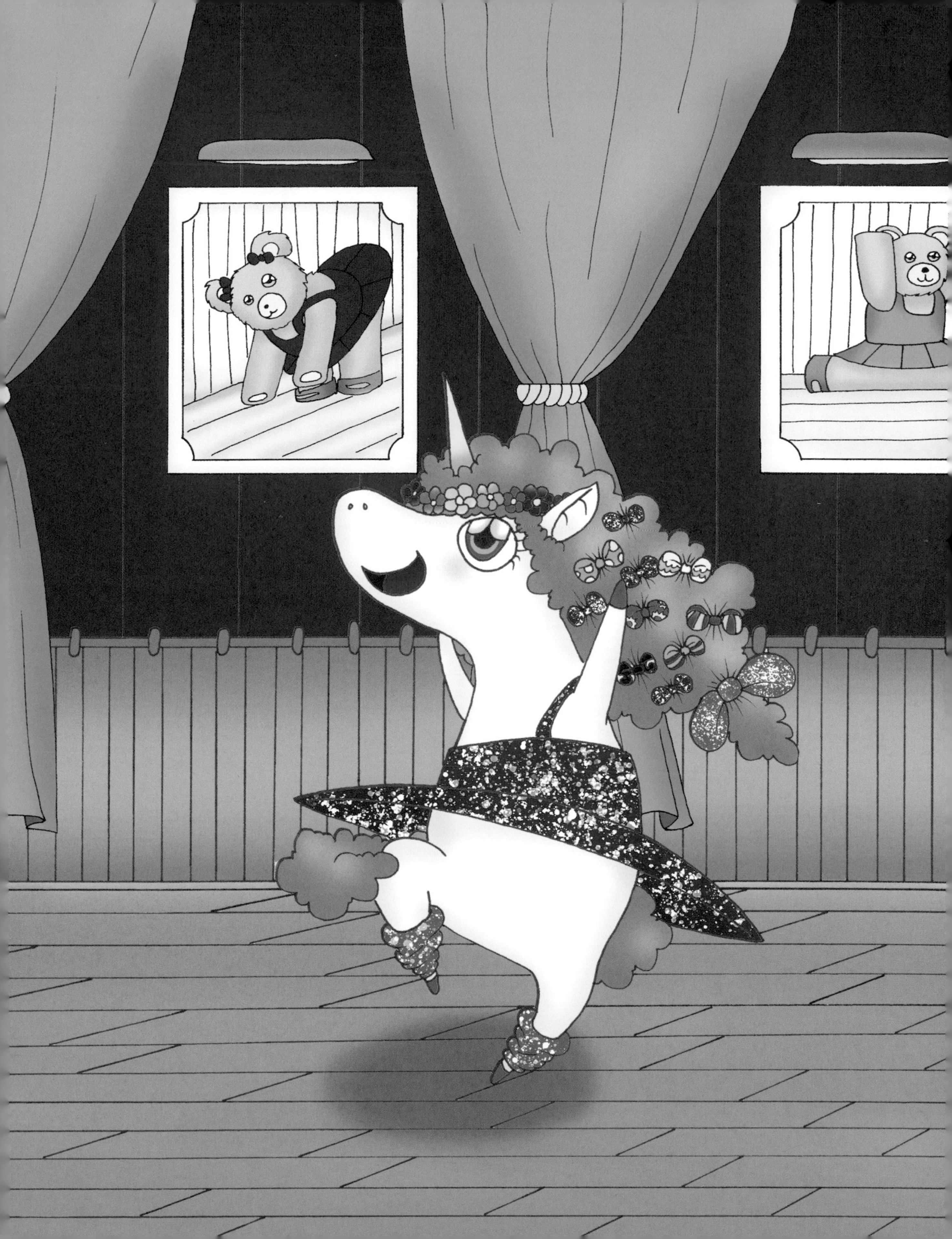

It was loads of fun for all until,
Qualms the Rabbit hopped in the room...
He looked at her with widened eyes,
His expression that of doom.

"This is an accident waiting to happen,"
His voice sounding austere...
"I would not tippy tap around like that,
For you could fall down in here."

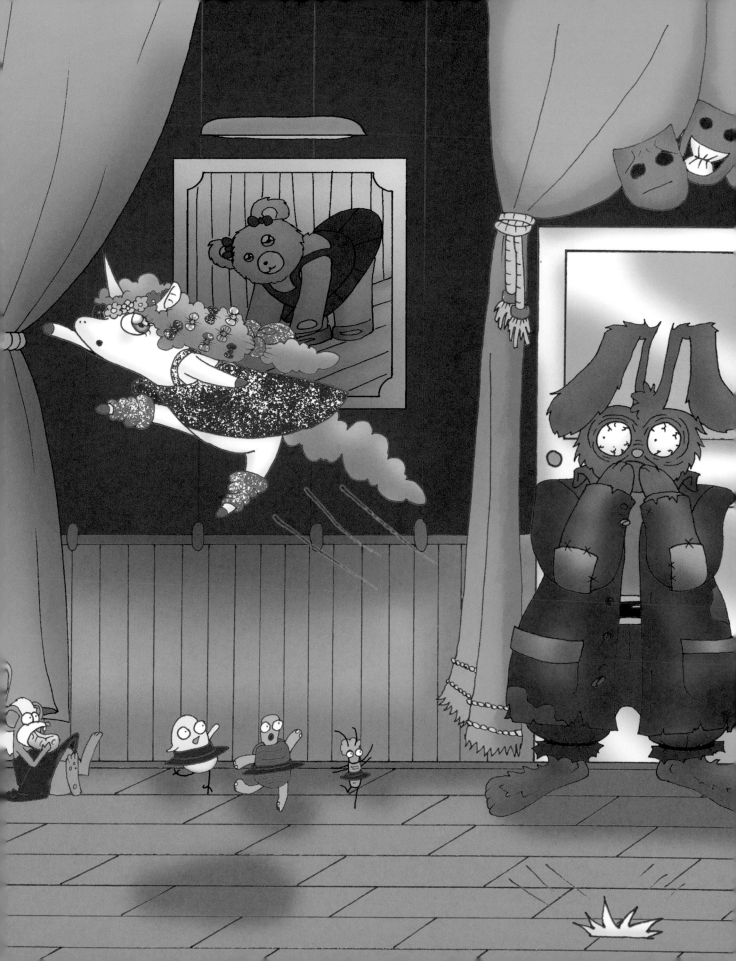

Another idea came to Reverie,
As she lay in bed that night...
"Maybe I don't need a storefront,
I just need to write!"

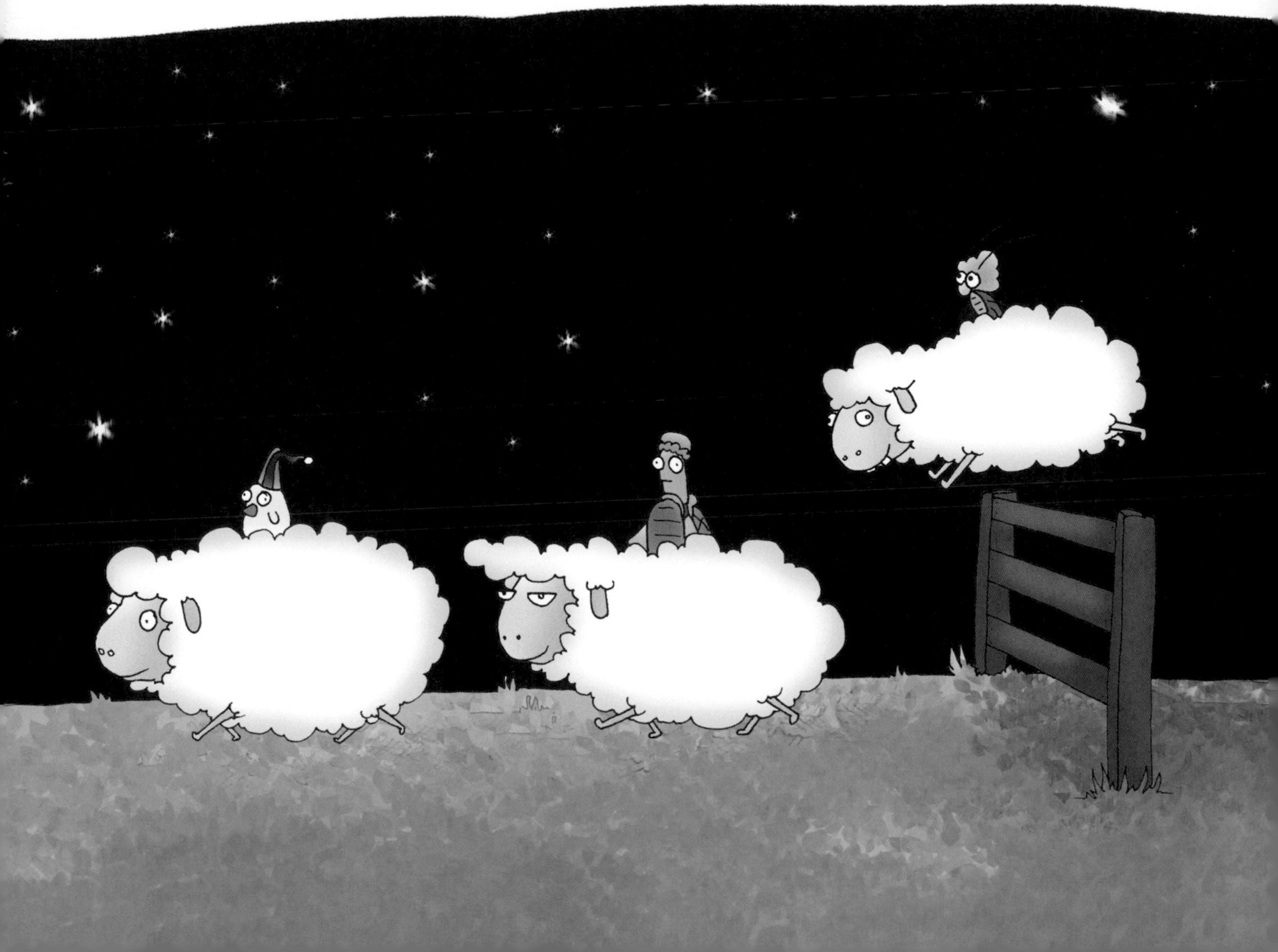

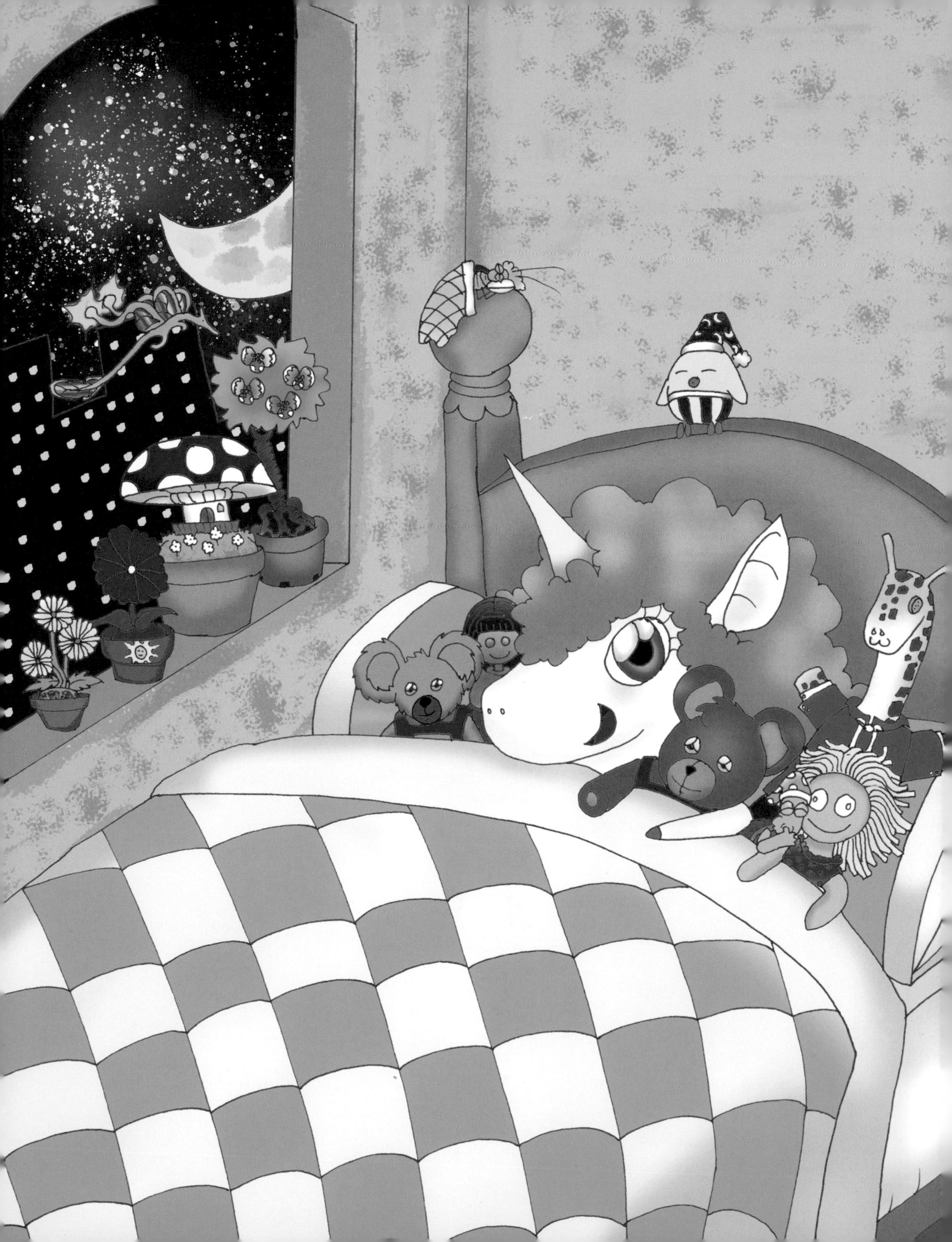

Her little hooves went cloppity click
On her trusty, old typewriter...
Ideas began to flow to her,
And the future looked much brighter.

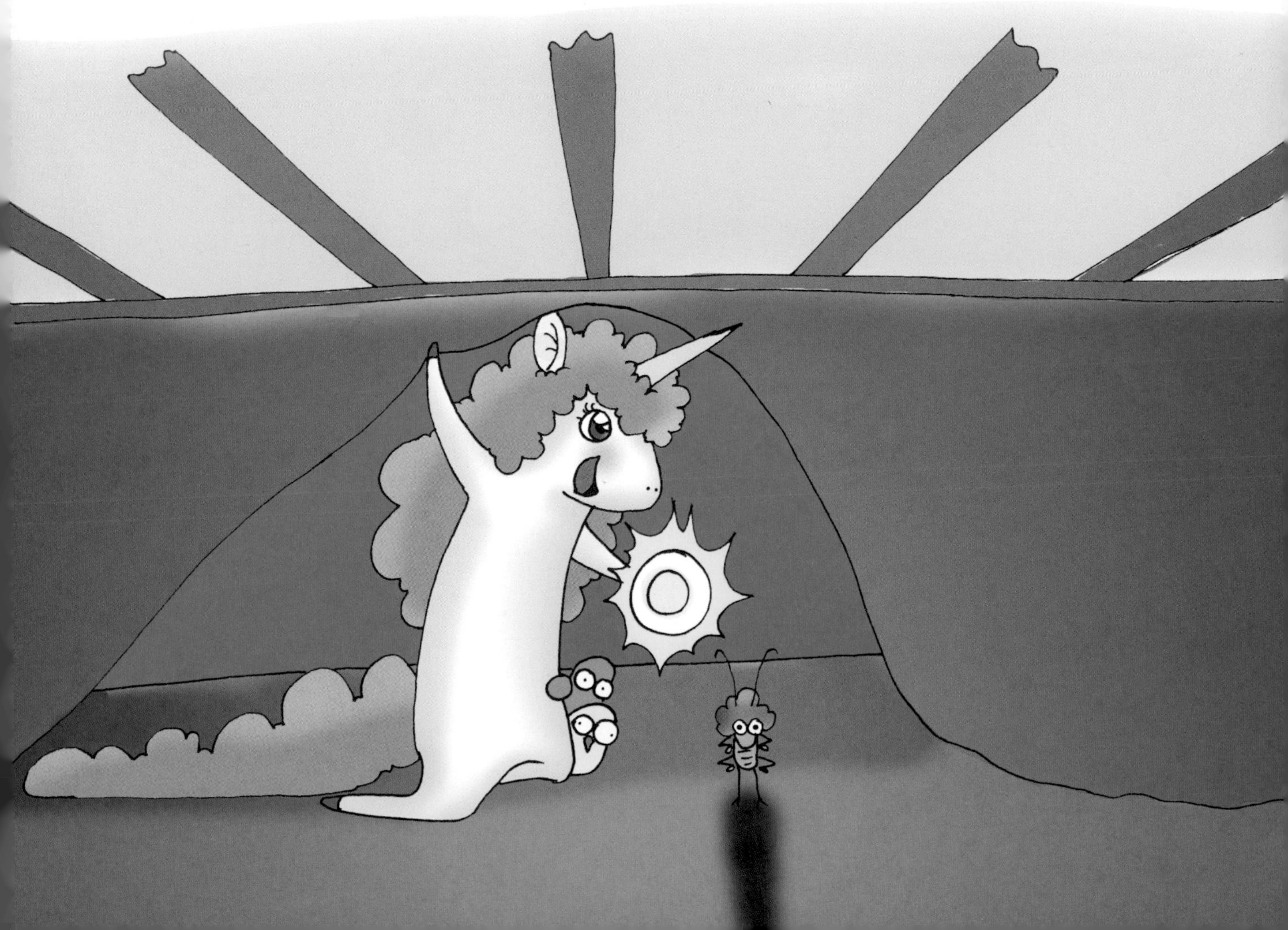

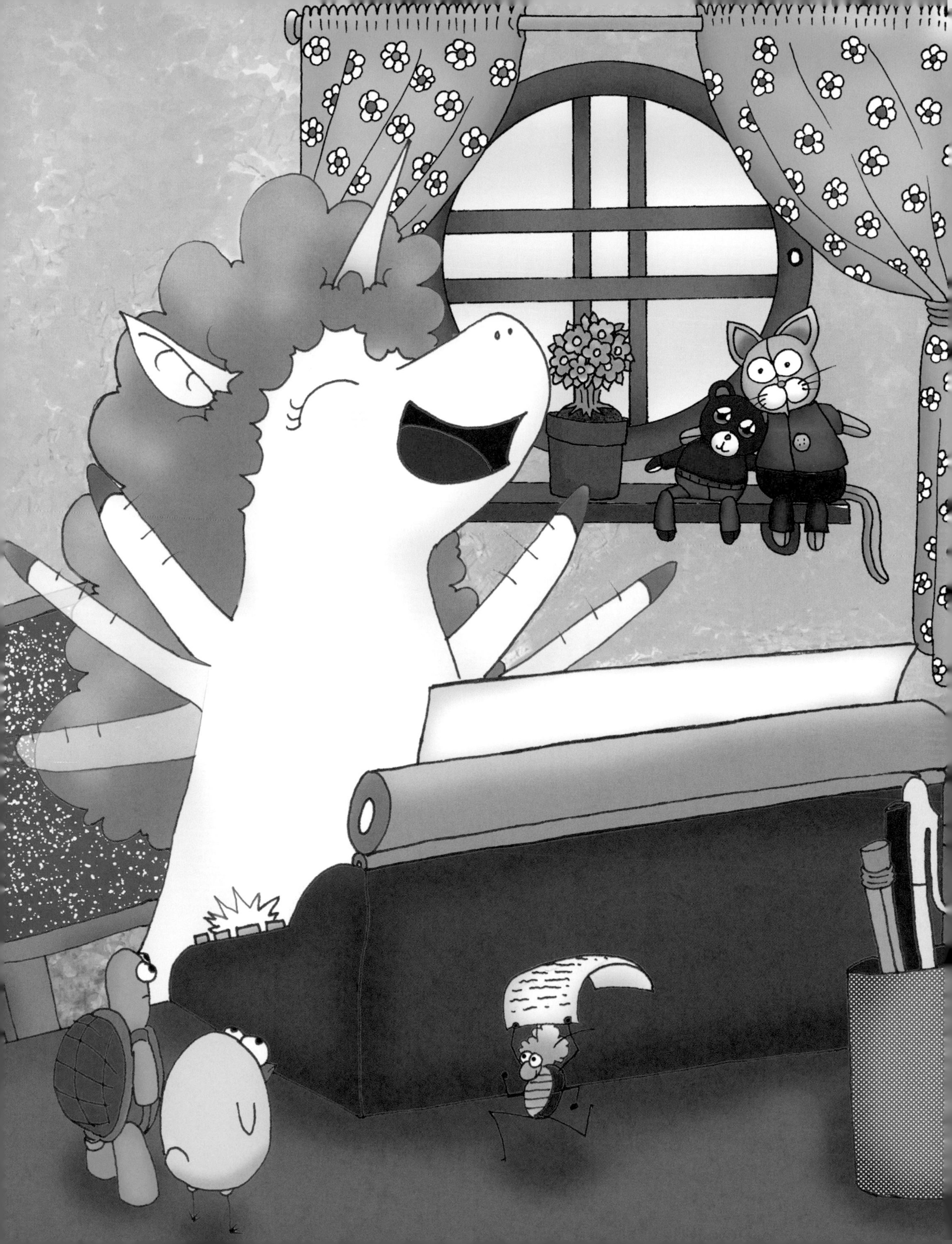

She sent her book away,
To see who it would please...
Rejection the Pig wrote a snooty review,
"This book's not worth a sneeze!"

"Give up writing now I say,
You are not the literary sort...
No one would buy a book like this,
Or offer their support!"

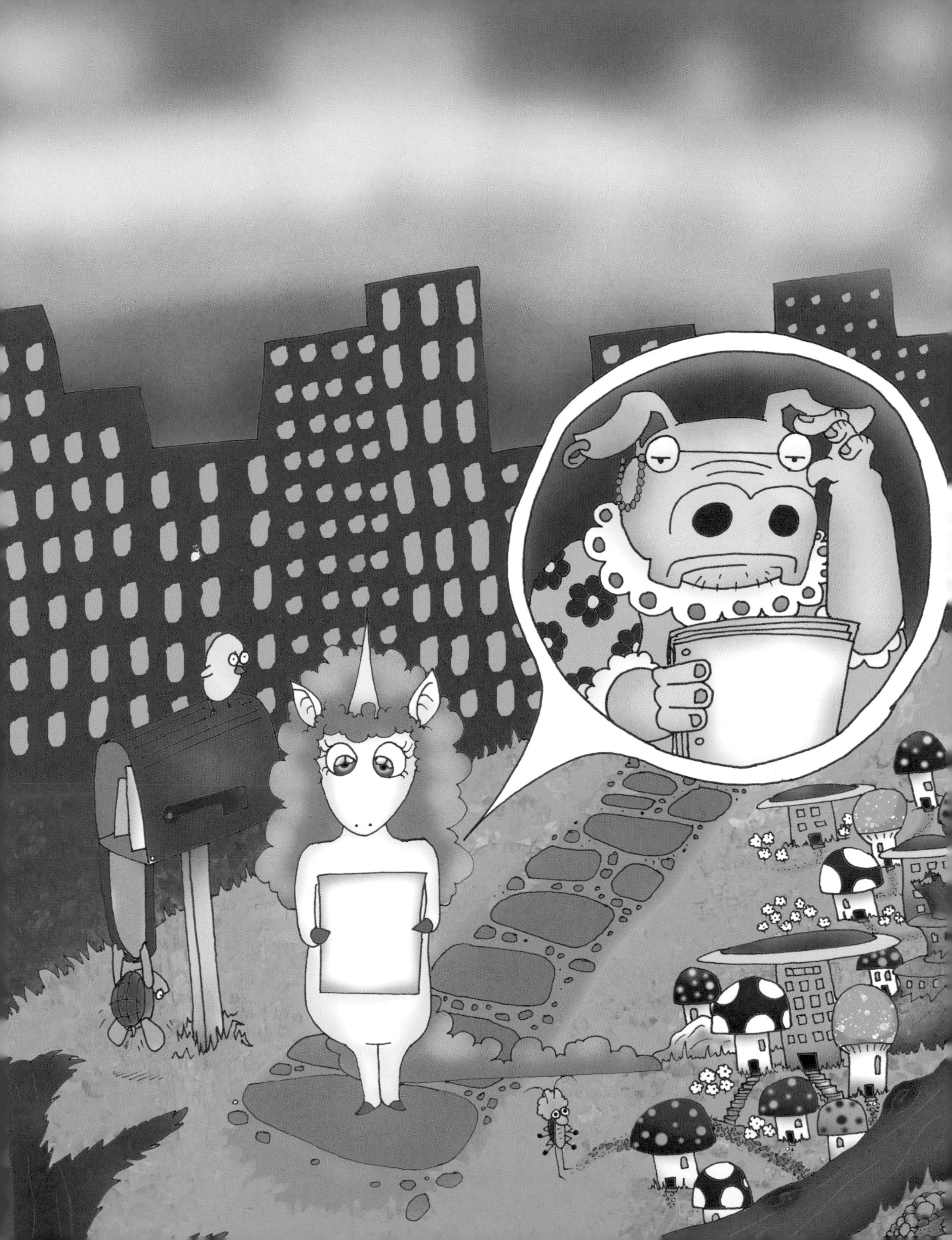

So Reverie, again, decided
To try out something new...
She had to keep on trying,
Anything would do.

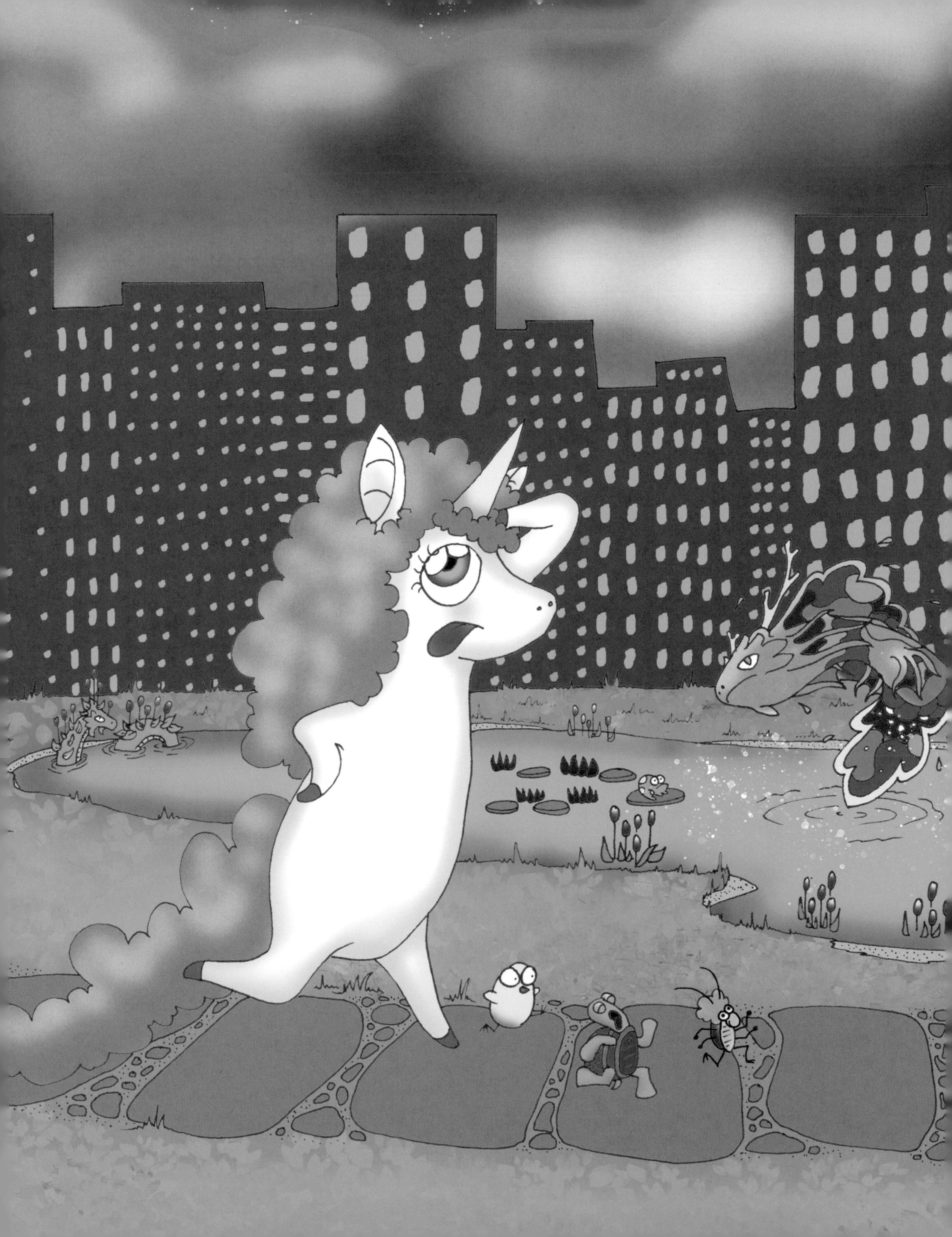

She opened up a garden shop,
Potting plants and watering seeds...
Her flowers would bloom so brightly,
And their beauty made her pleased.

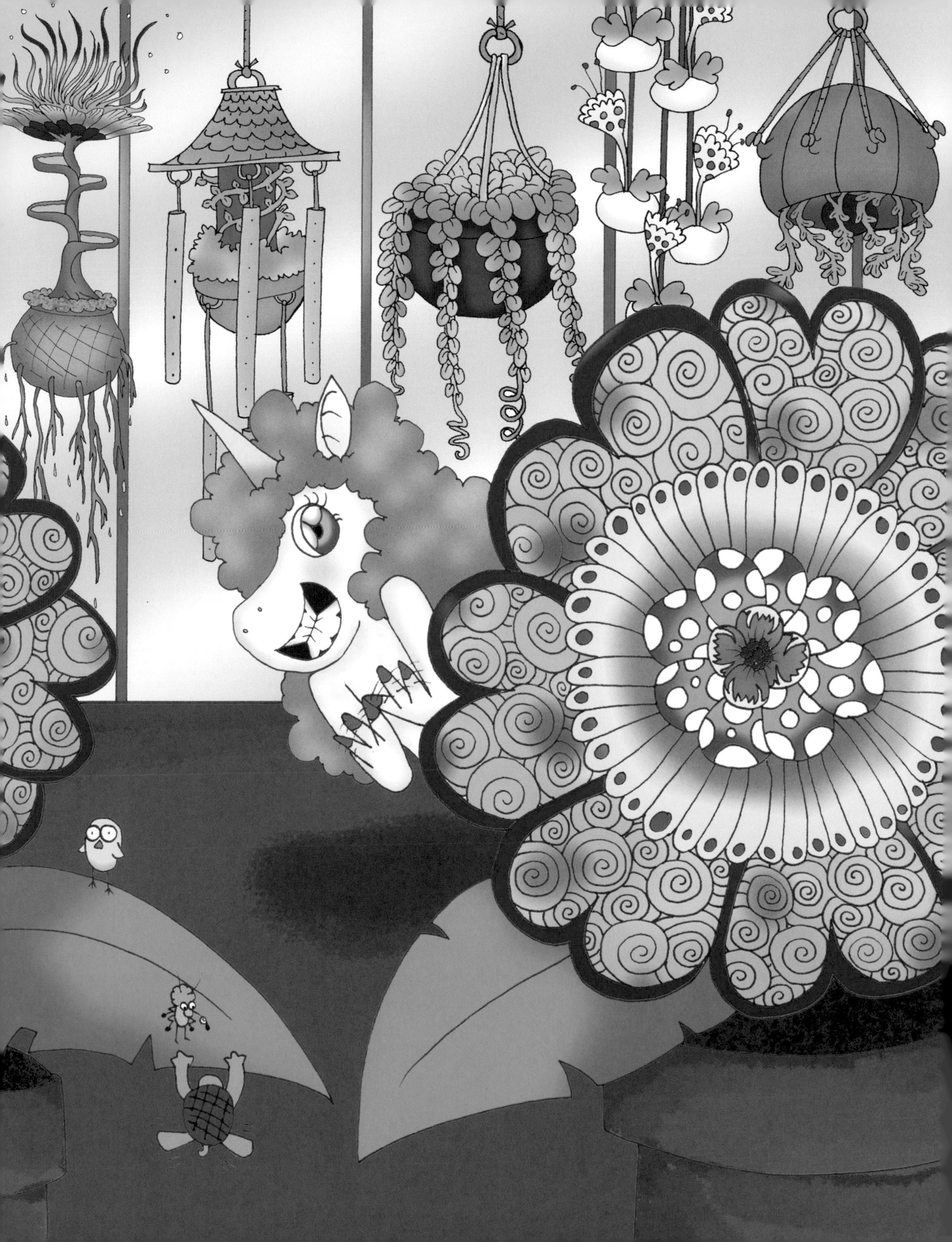

Intimidation the Bear stomped in,
And growled at her endeavor...
"Anyone can plant a seed,
You really aren't that clever."

"Give up!" he scorned, "Give me your shop,
For I can make it succeed."
"Go get a job like a normal creature!
For that is all you need."

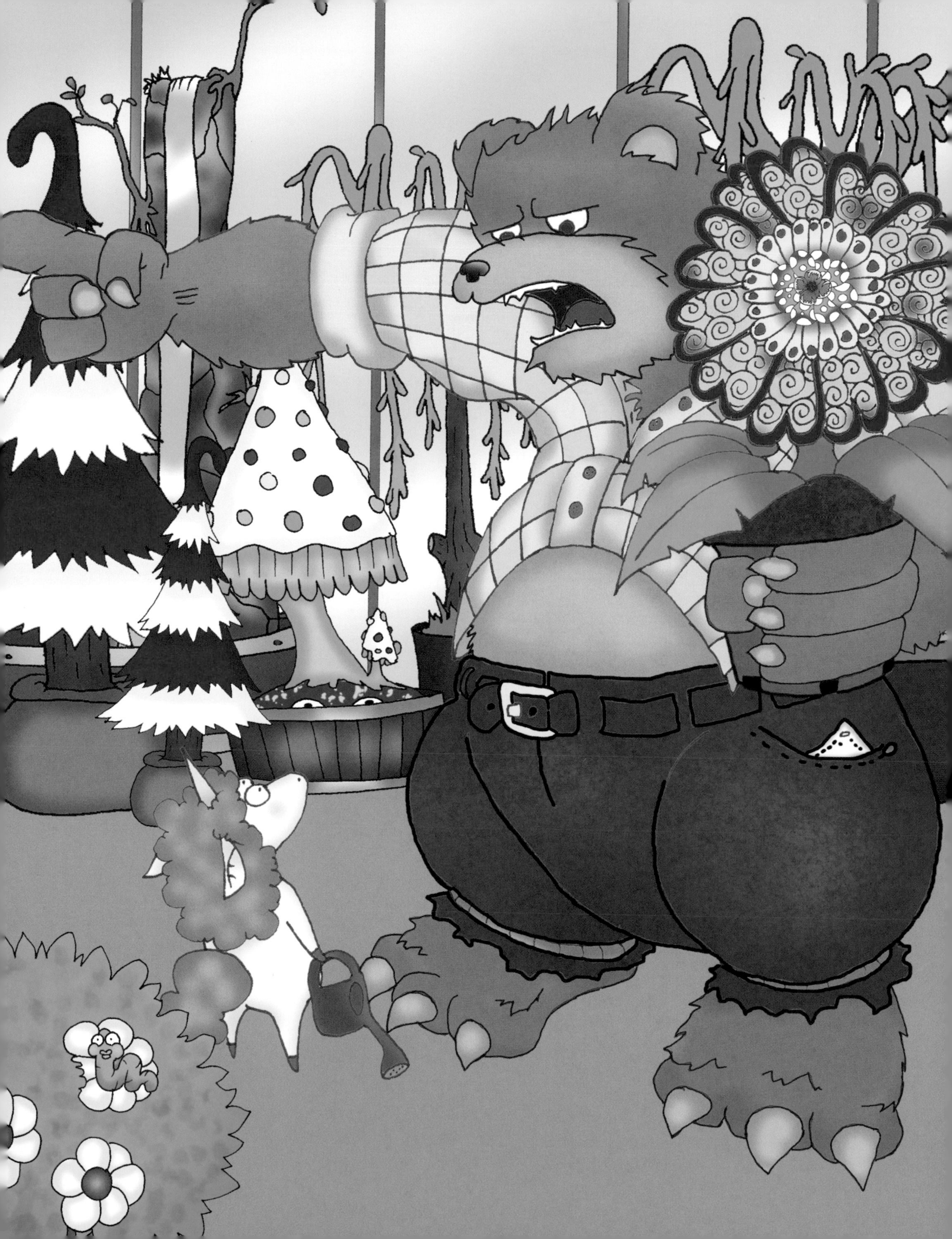

No one believes in unicorns,
To Reverie, it was clear...
She got a job, worked day and night,
And worked for about a year.

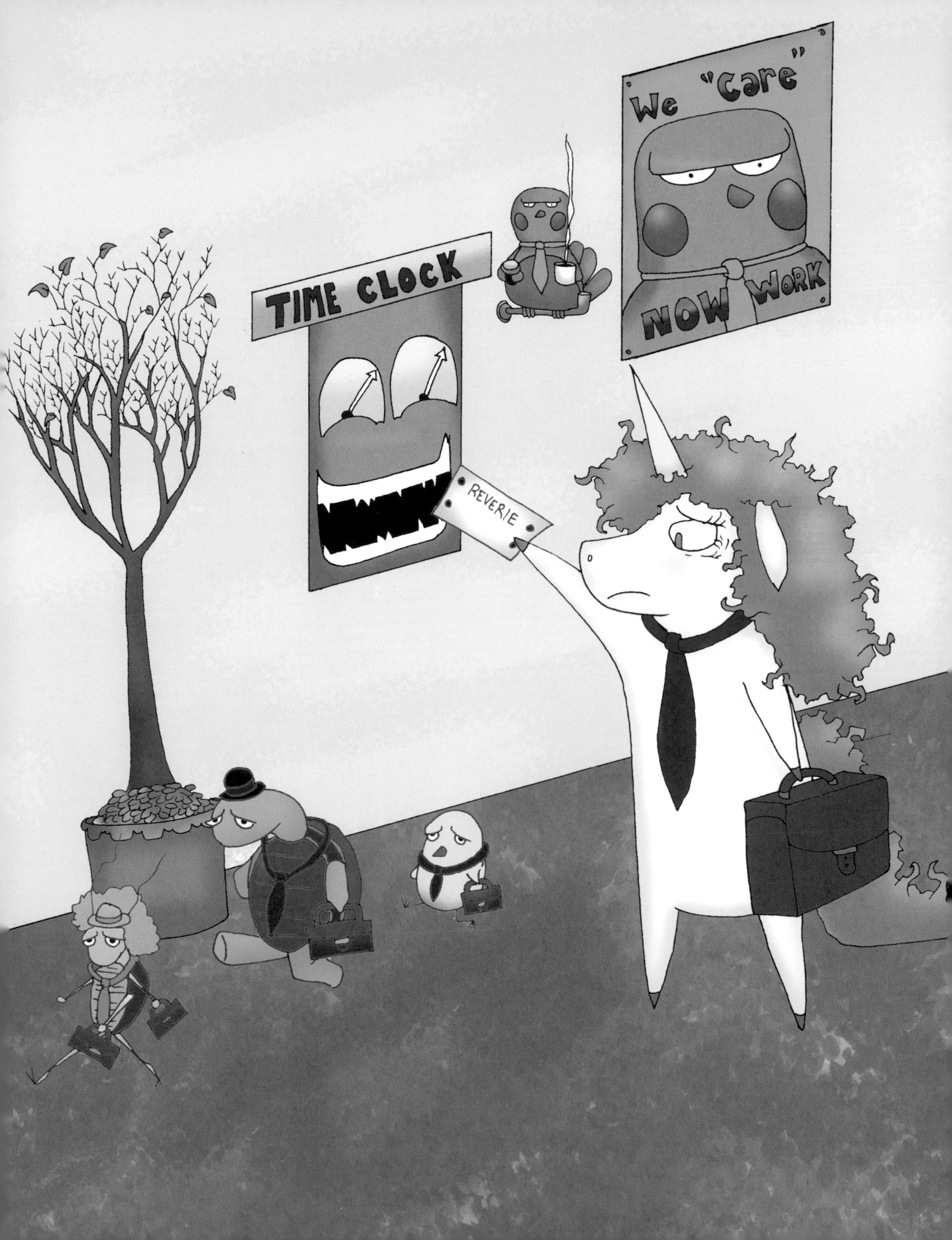
We "Care"
NOW WORK
TIME CLOCK
REVERIE

Her little hooves typed in data,
A cubicle is where she stayed...
The sparkle left her tired eyes,
And her countenance dismayed.

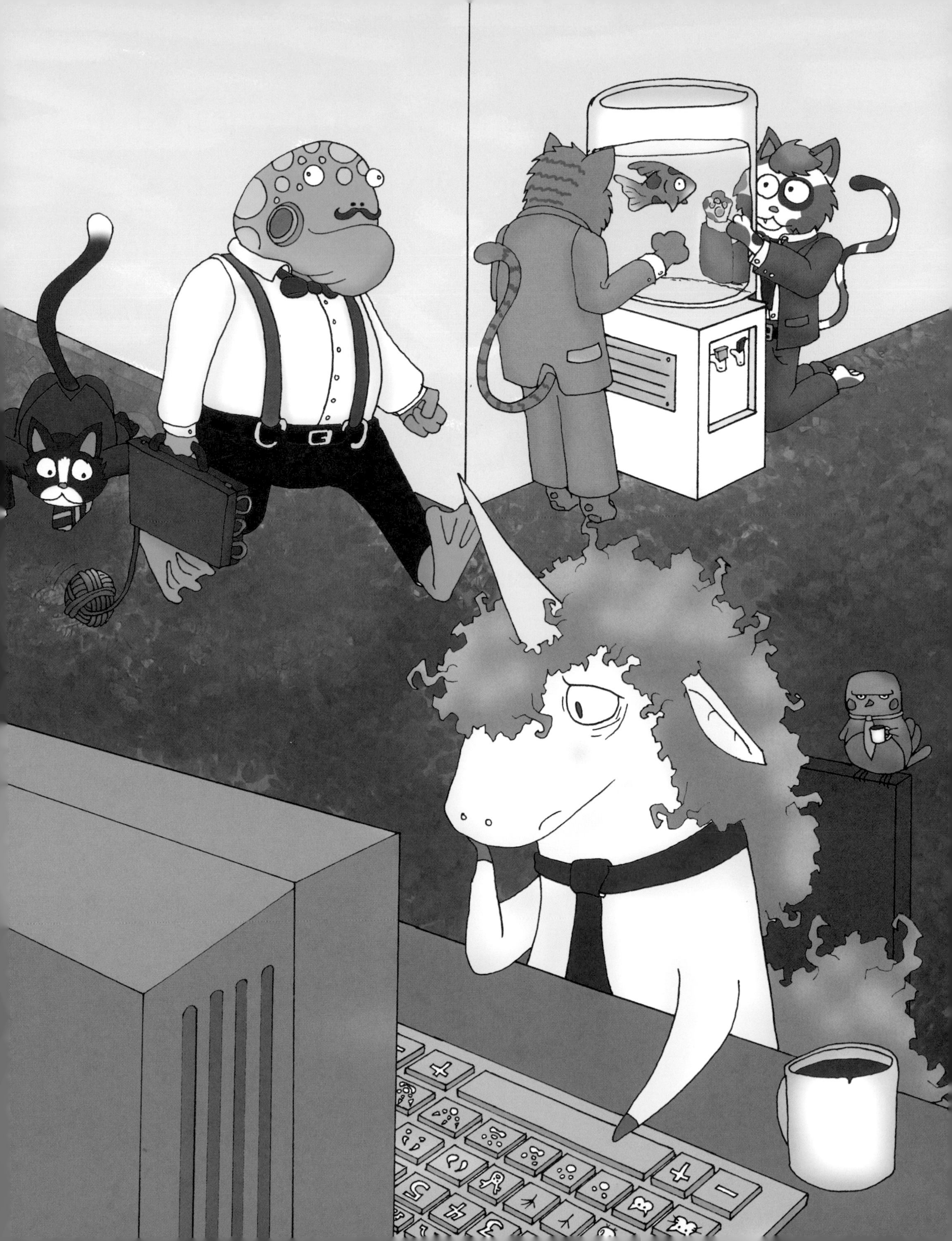

Discontent the Sprite leaned in,
"Reverie, why are you so sad?"
"If working here is not what you love,
Then do what makes you glad."

"I've tried so very hard,
To make my dreams reality...
But no matter what it was I did,
No one would believe in me."

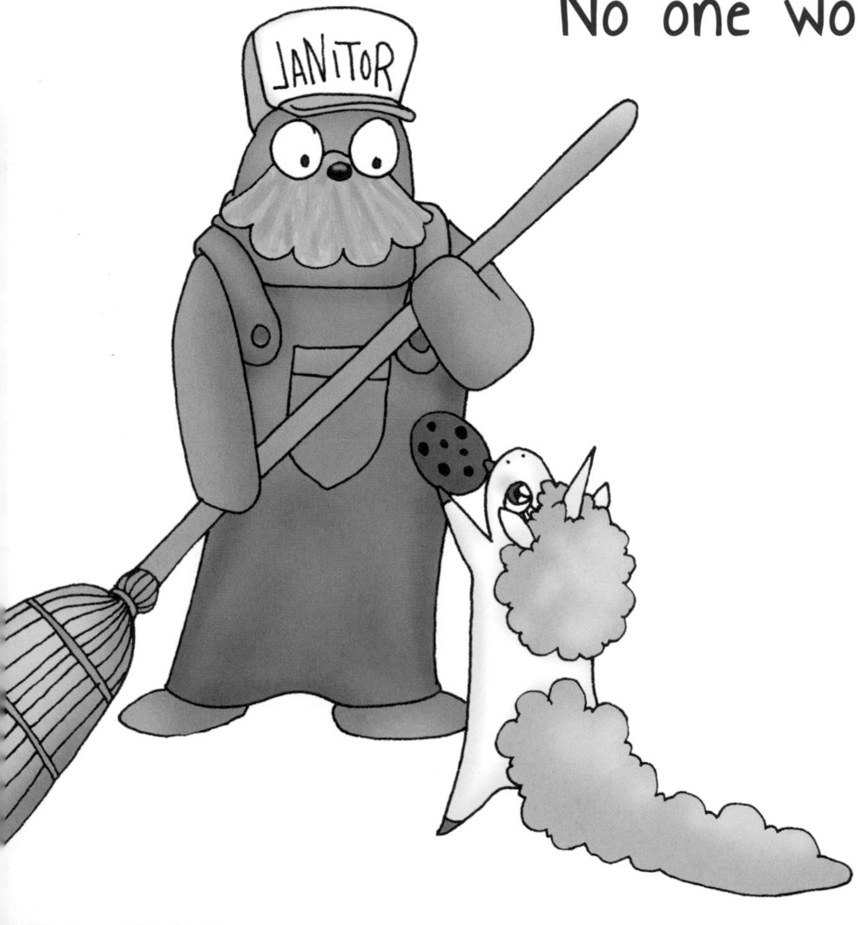
JANITOR

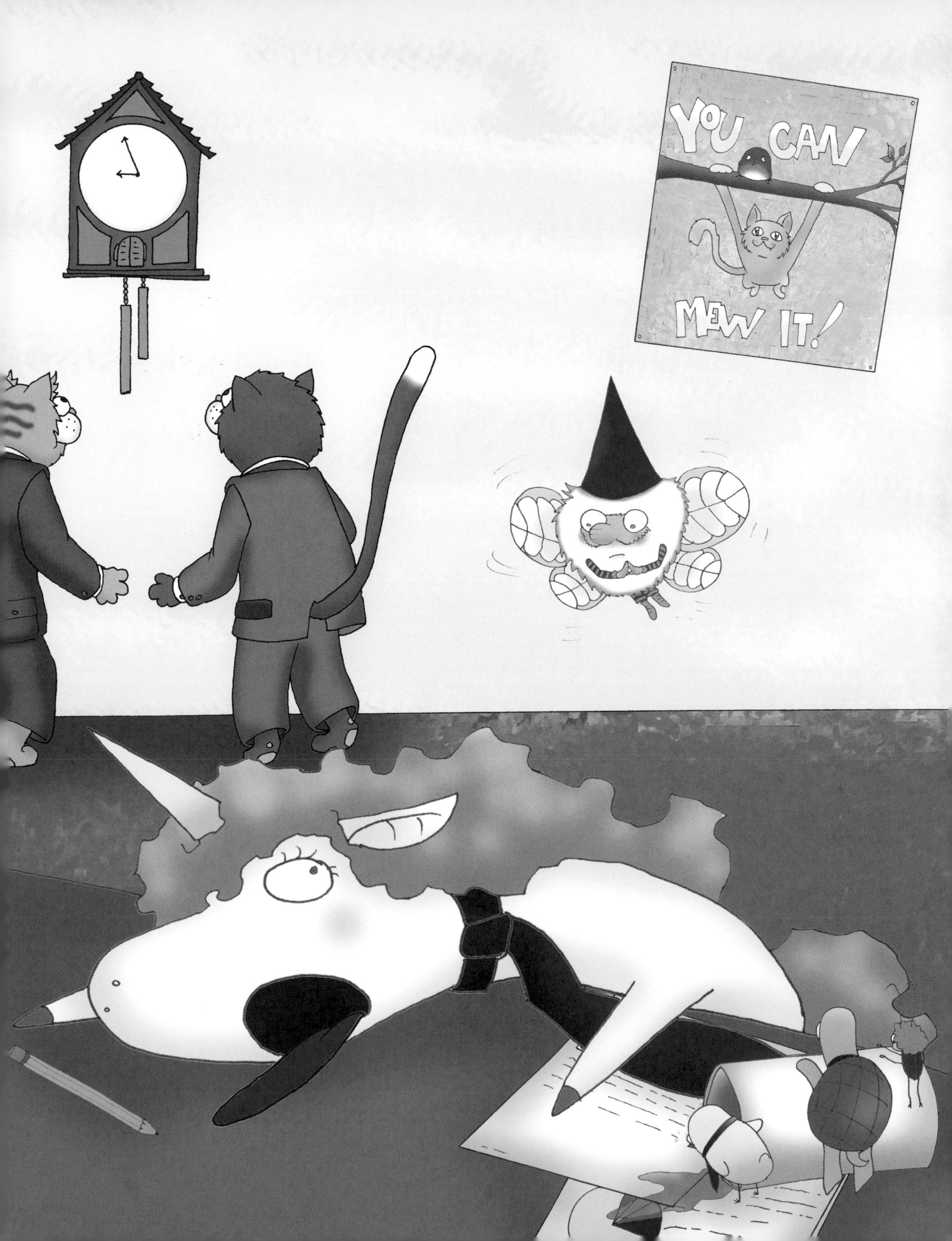

YOU CAN
MEW IT!

Discontent gave out a sigh,
And tugged her cotton-candy mane...
"Believe in YOURSELF, dear Reverie,
For you have so much to gain."

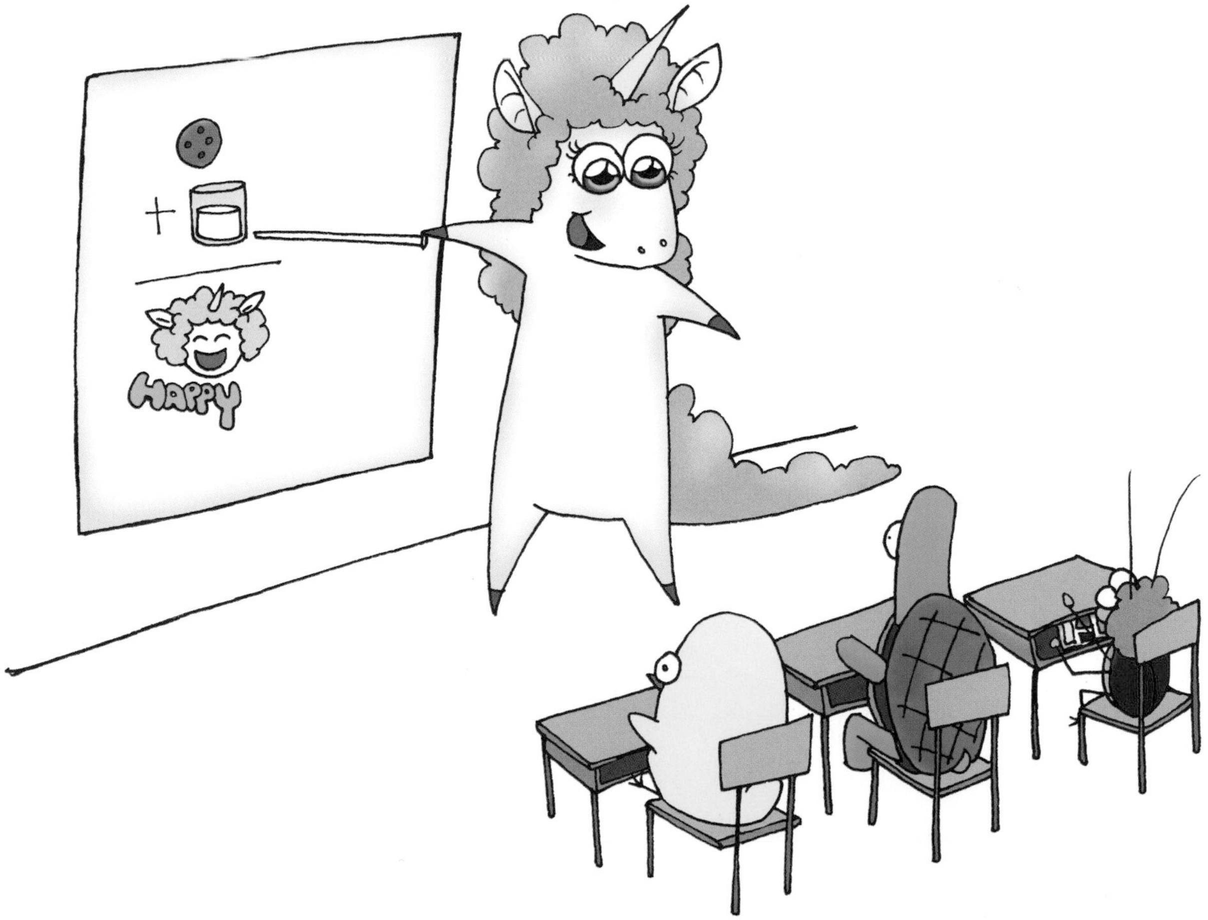
HAPPY

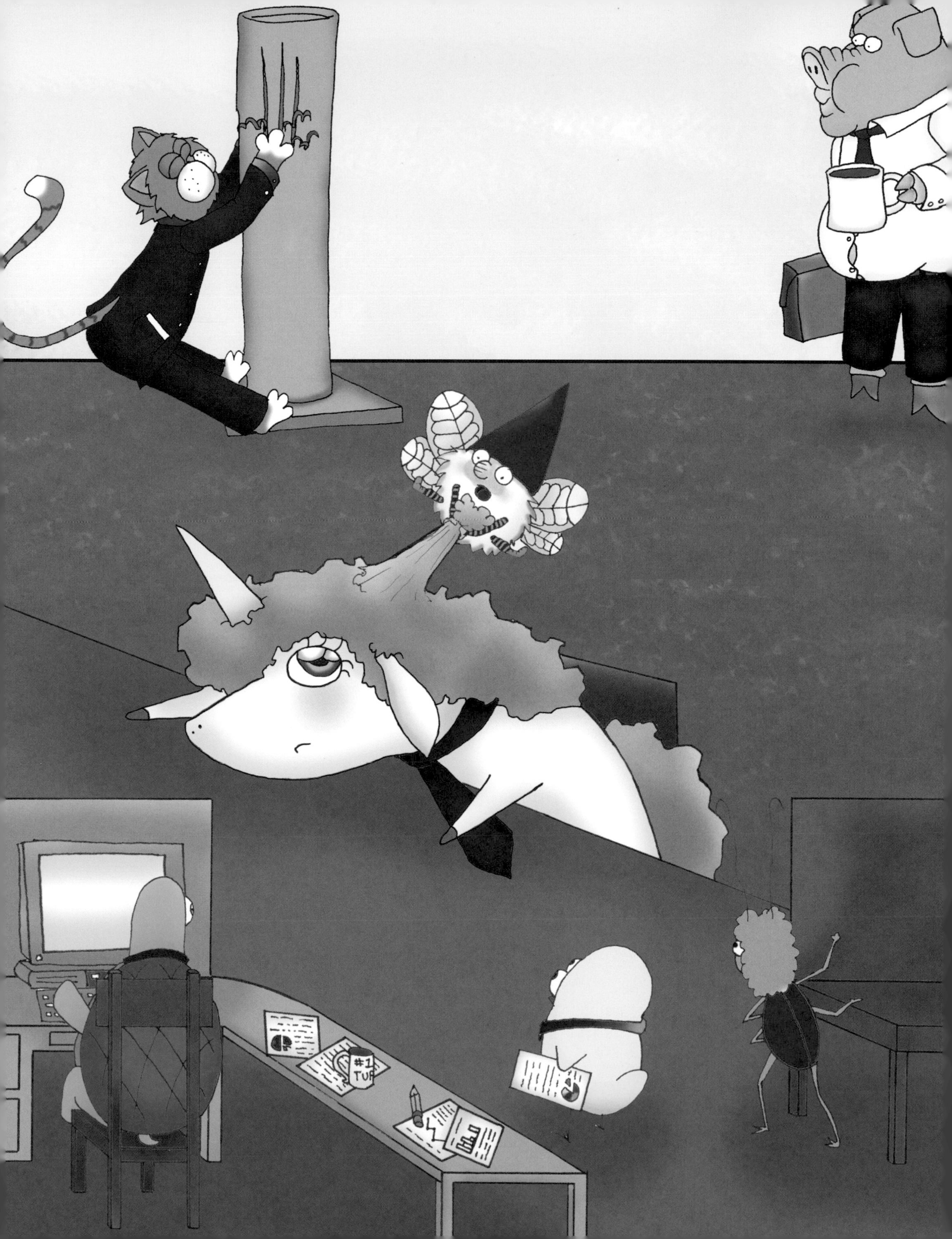
#1
TUR

"You gave up too soon, my precious friend,
Believing other's lies...
If you work hard and believe in yourself,
Any dreams can be realized."

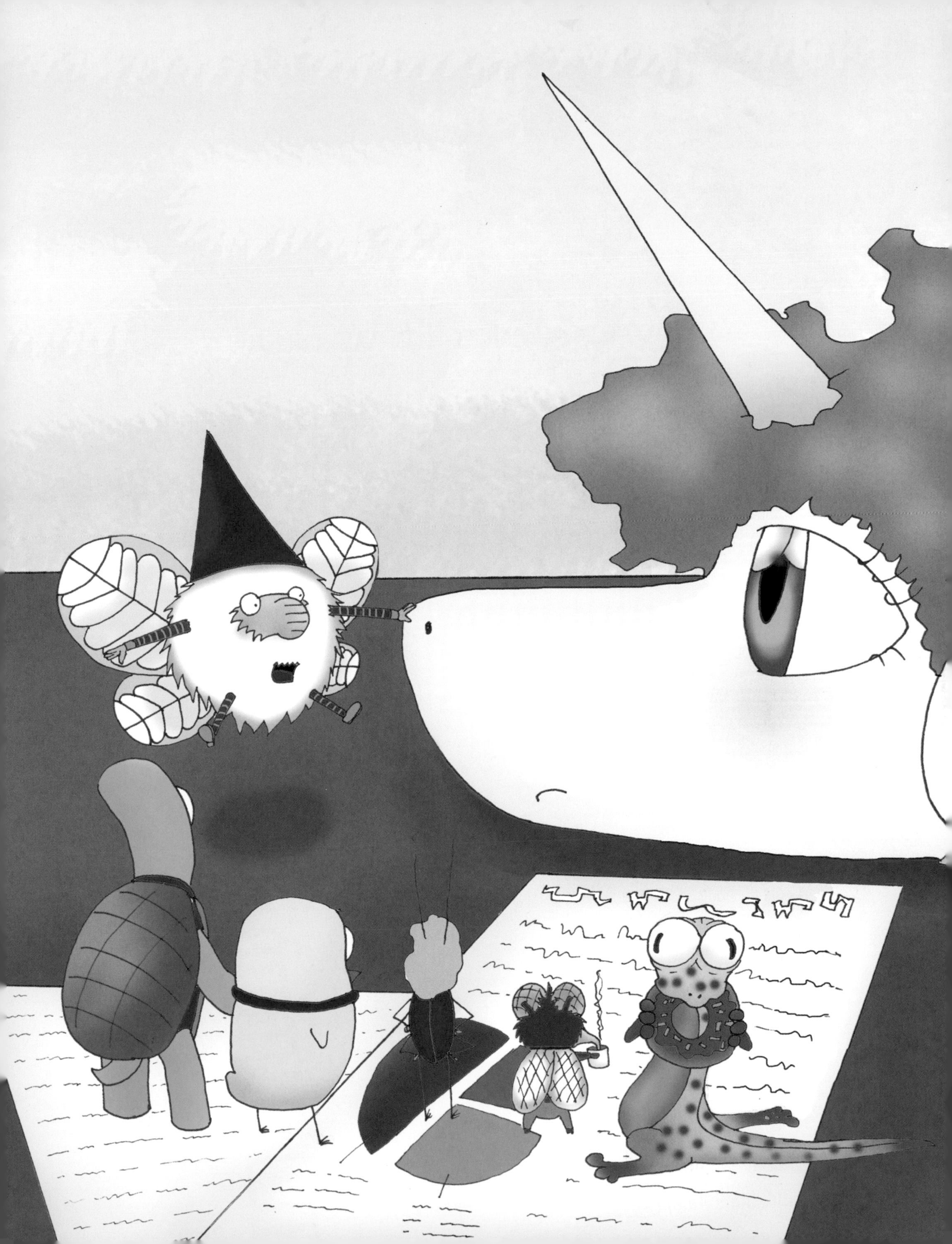

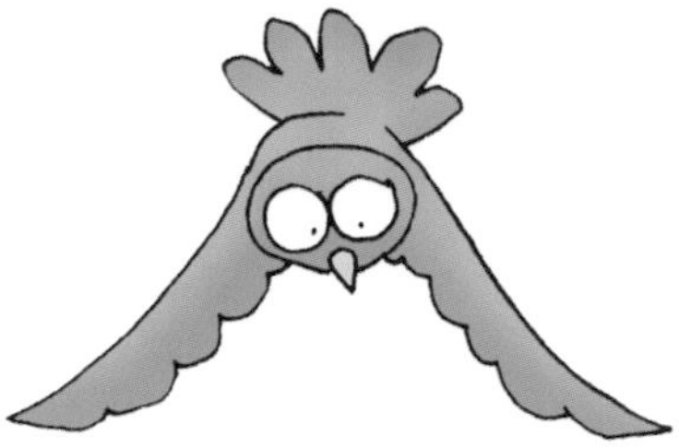

Reverie's eyes lit up again,
With sparkle and delight...
She lept up on her office desk,
"Thank you, friend! You're right!"

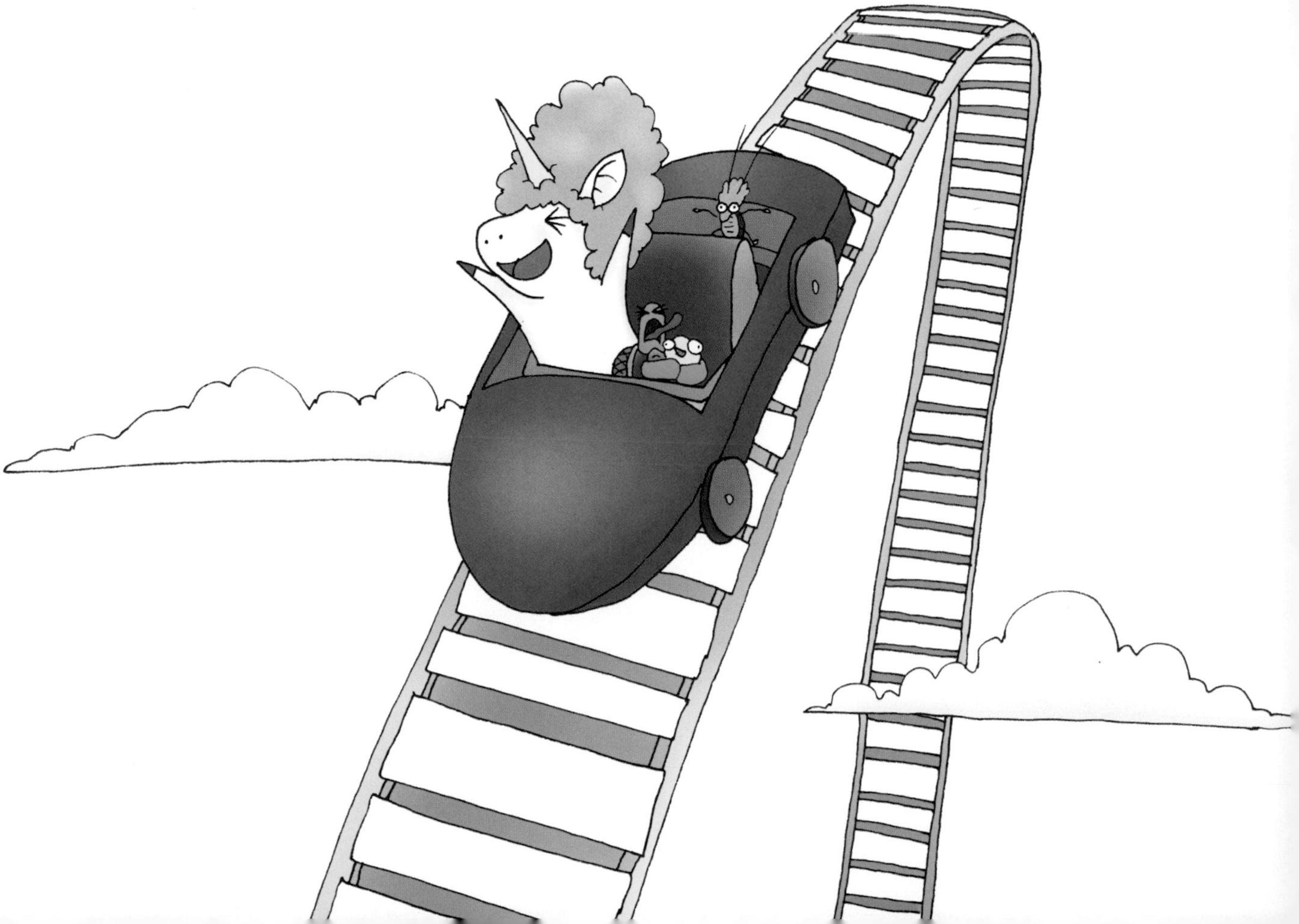

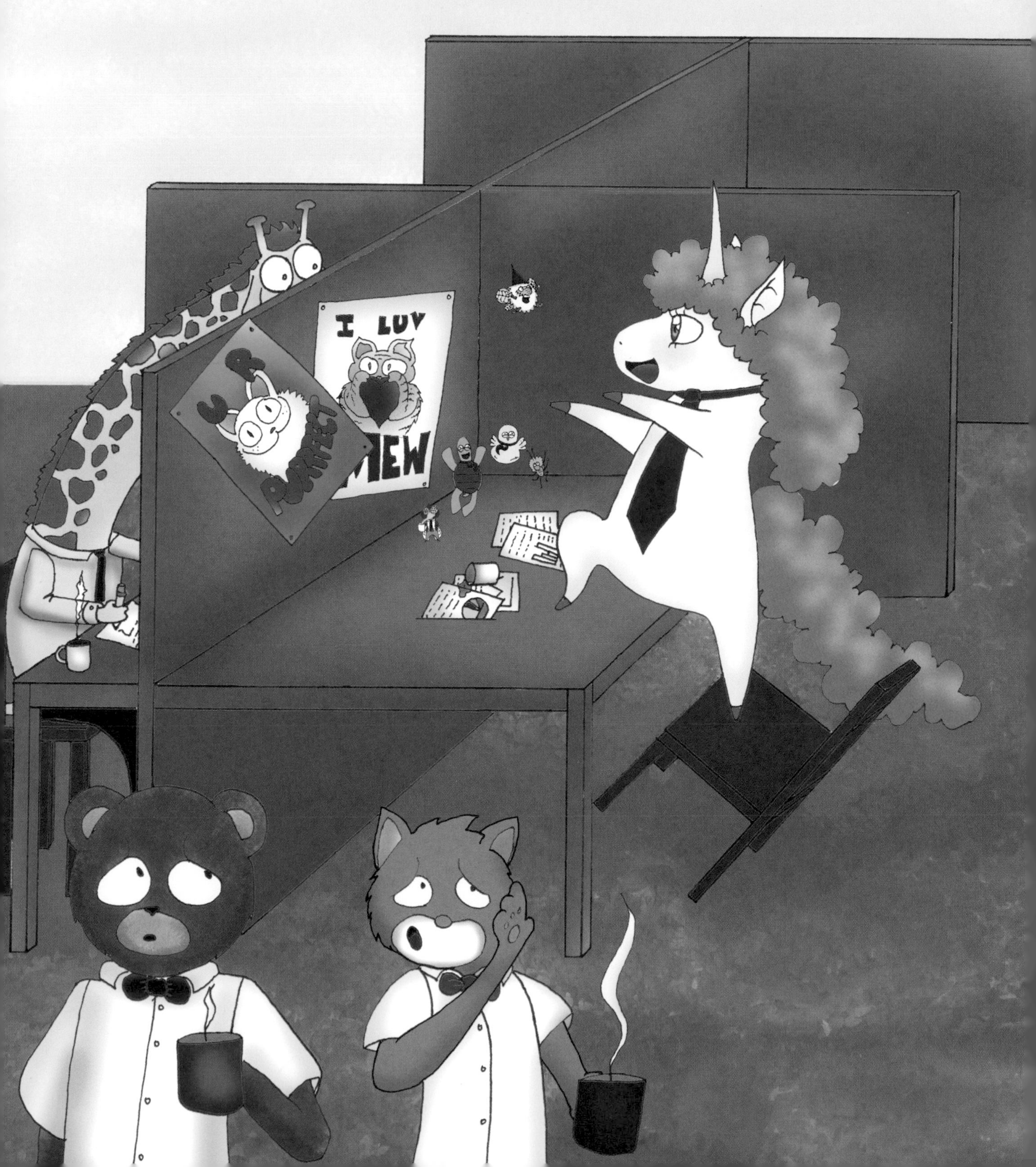

I LUV
MEW
U R
PURRFECT

"I forgot the most important thing,
In my efforts to achieve...
I let self-doubt tell me what to do,
When I just needed to believe!"

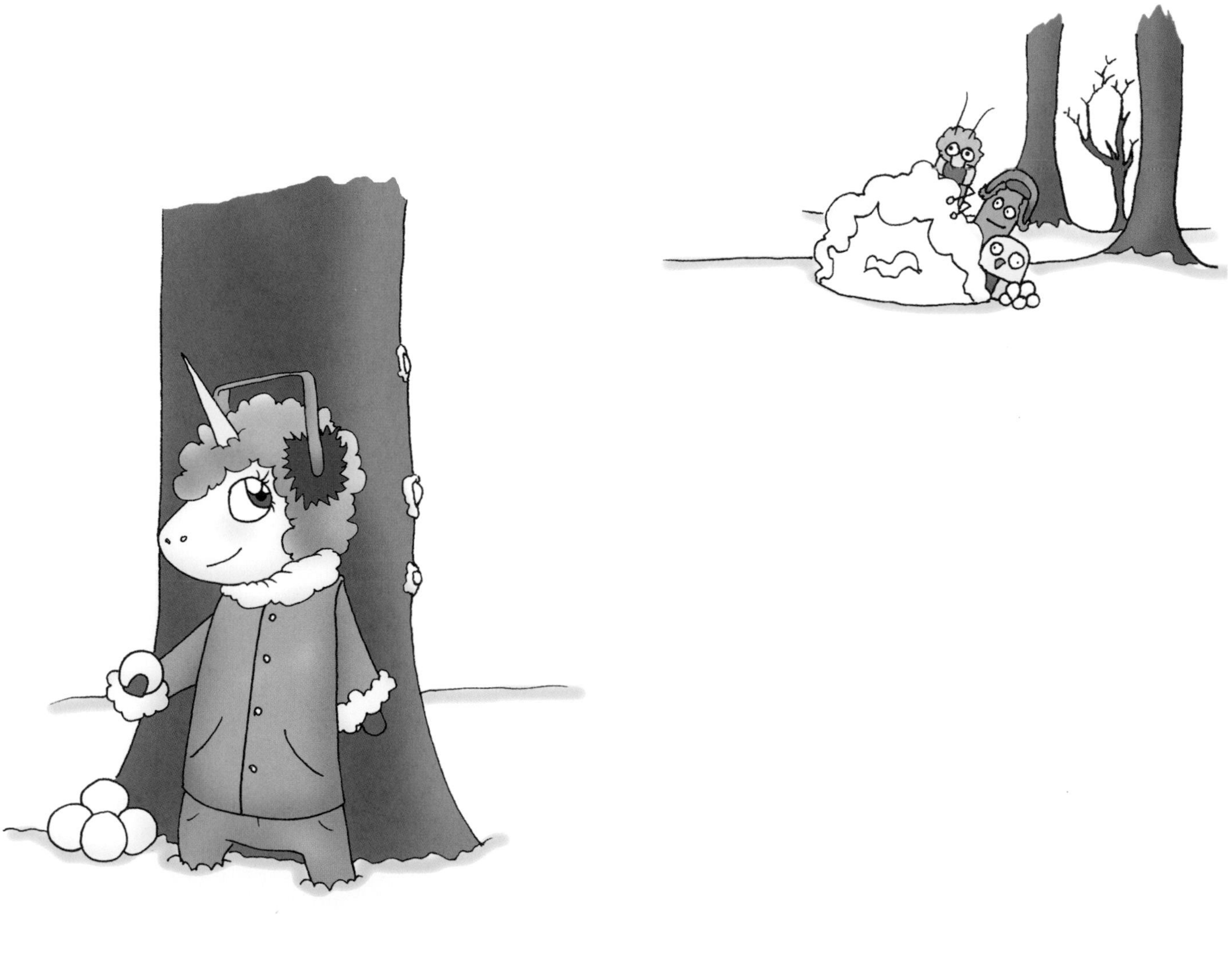

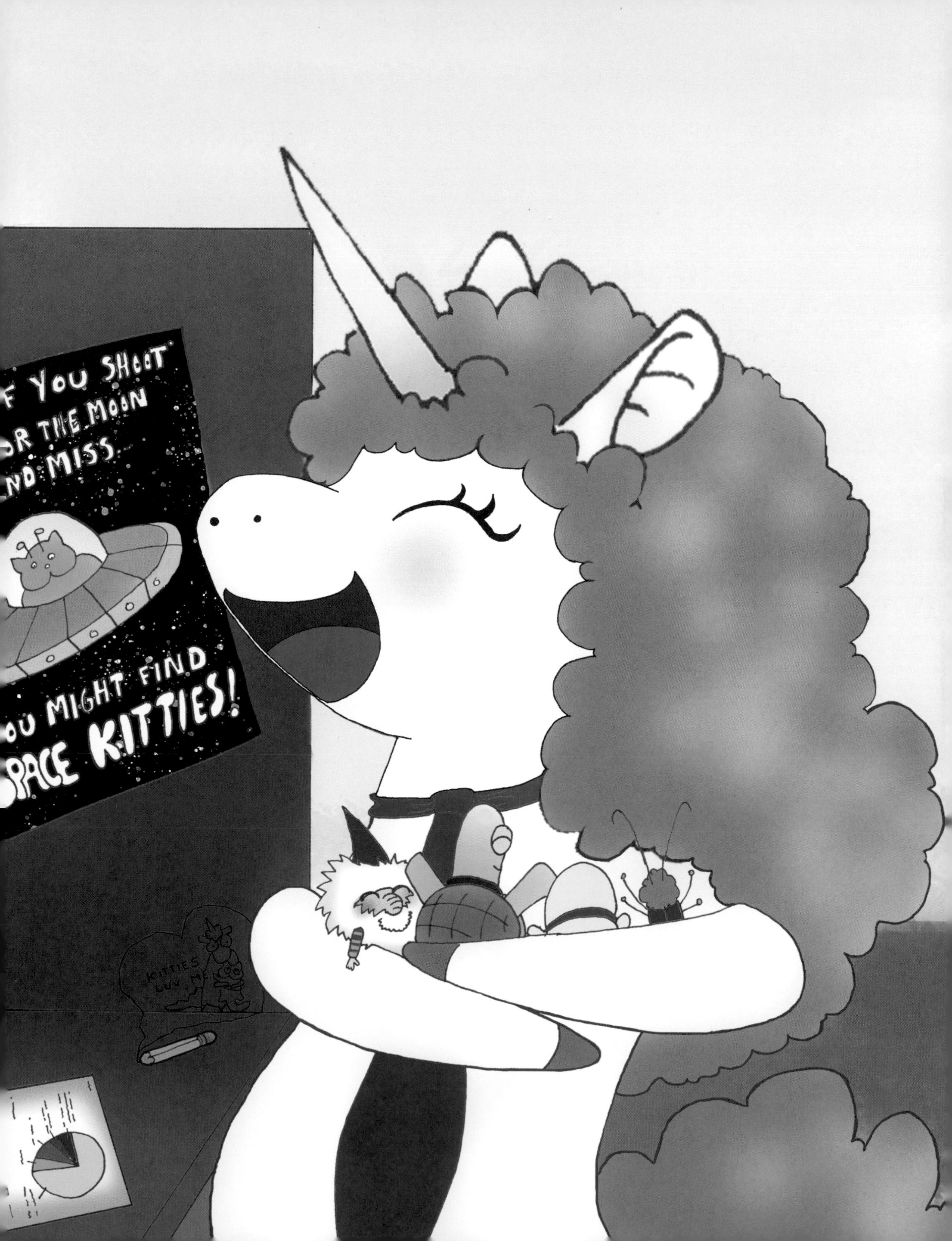
F YOU SHOOT
OR THE MOON
ND MISS
OU MIGHT FIND
PACE KITTIES!
KITTIES LUV ME

Reverie reopened her bakery,
She sold out of stock each day...
Her sweets were so unique and yummy,
People lined up outside to pay.

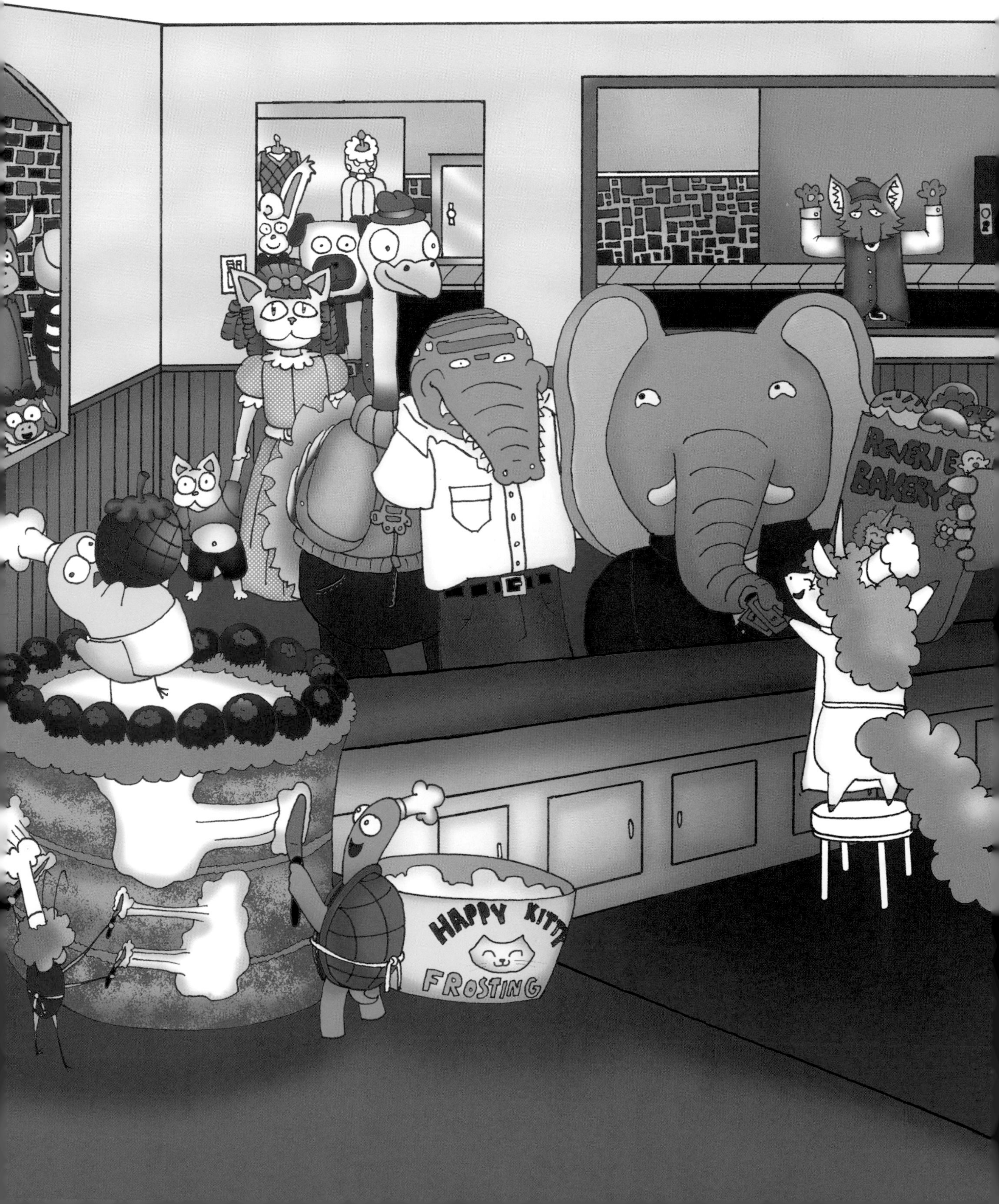
REVERIE BAKERY
HAPPY KITTY
FROSTING

Her hair salon gained such renown,
From everyone that she made pretty...
It quickly became the most popular place
to get your hair done in the city.

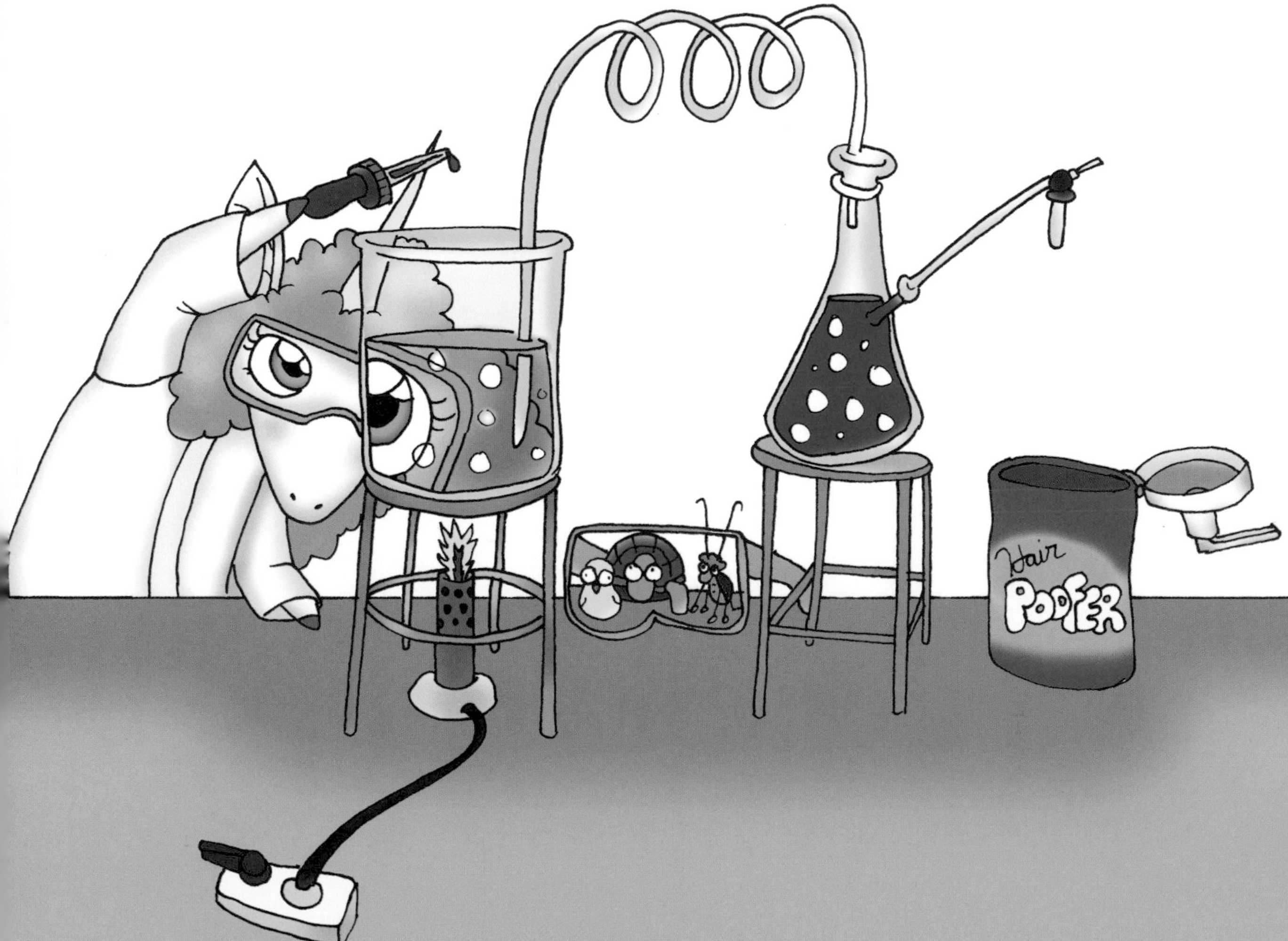
Hair
POOFER

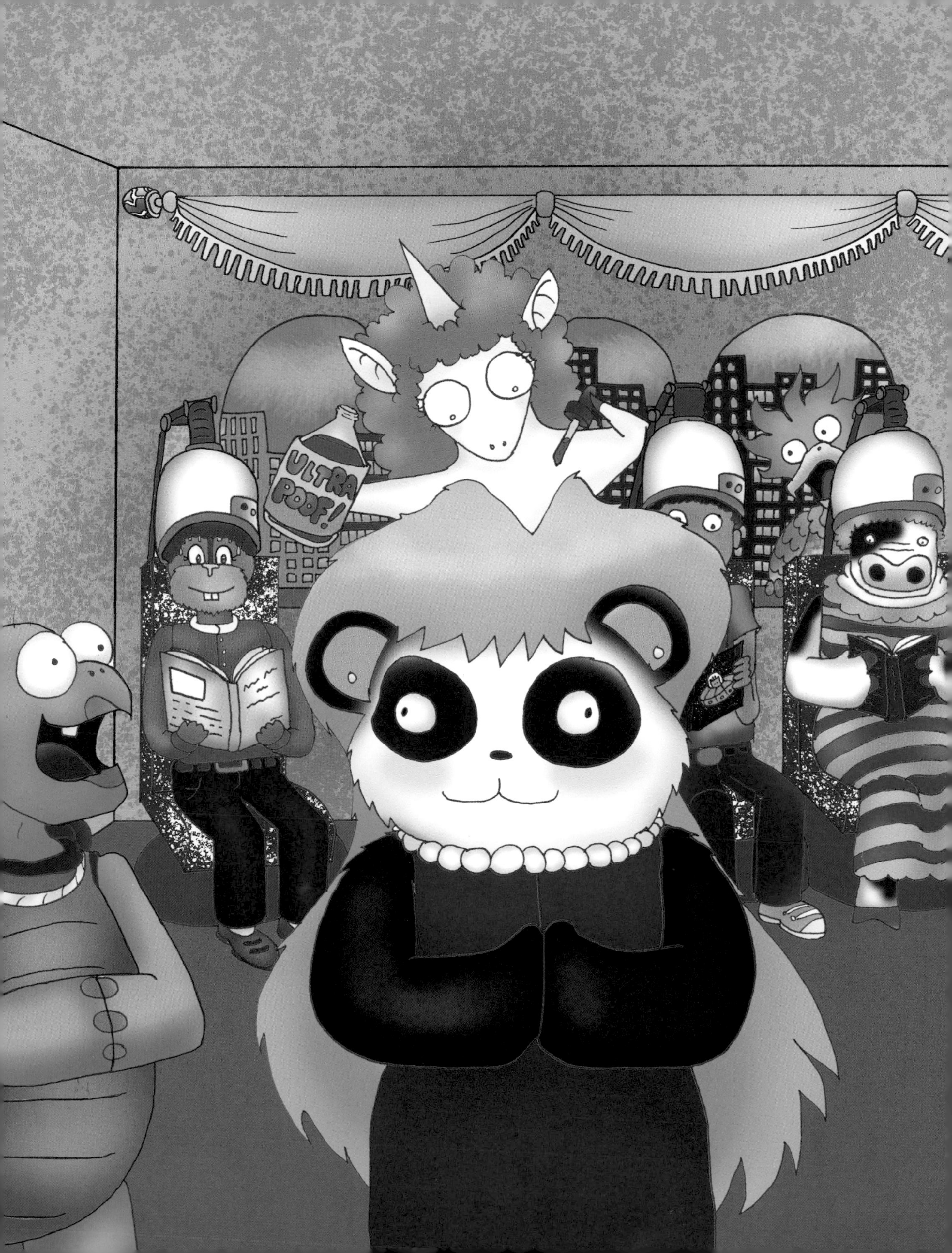
ULTRA POOF!

Her little hooves did tippy-tap
As she danced around and twirled...
She taught so many others too,
She became known around the world!

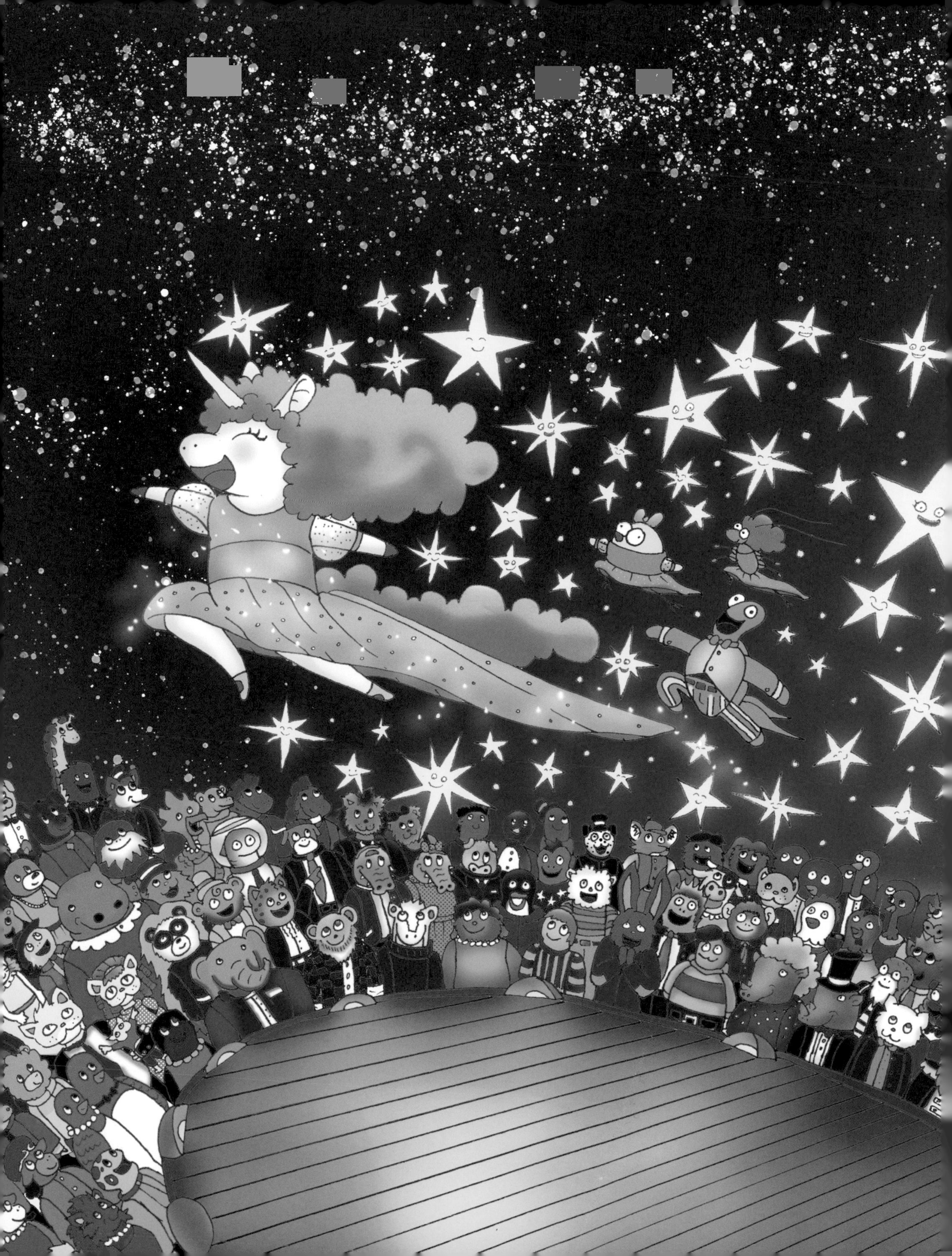

She turned her little hooves around,
And wrote that novel from before...
And this time people noticed it,
And begged her to write more!

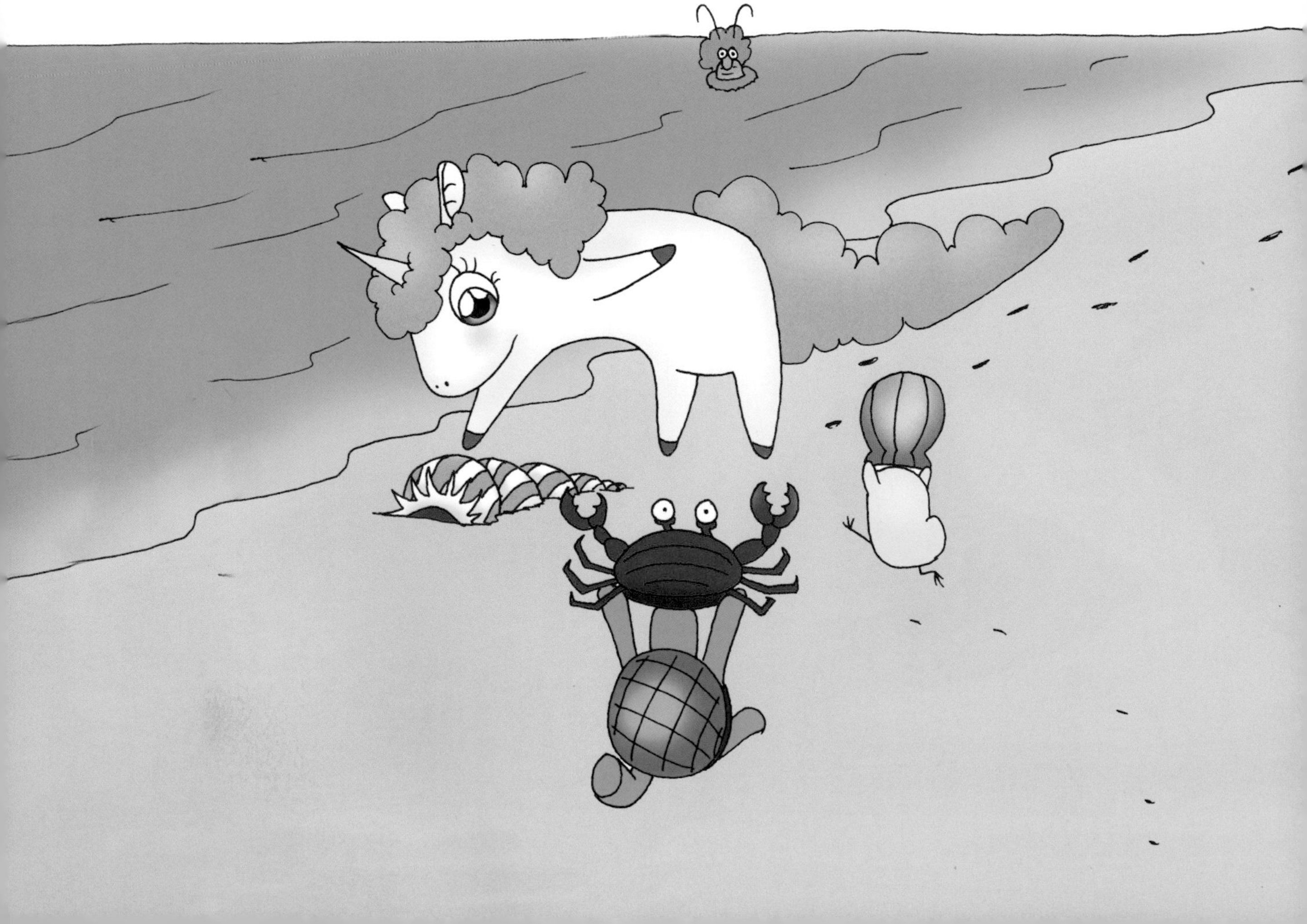

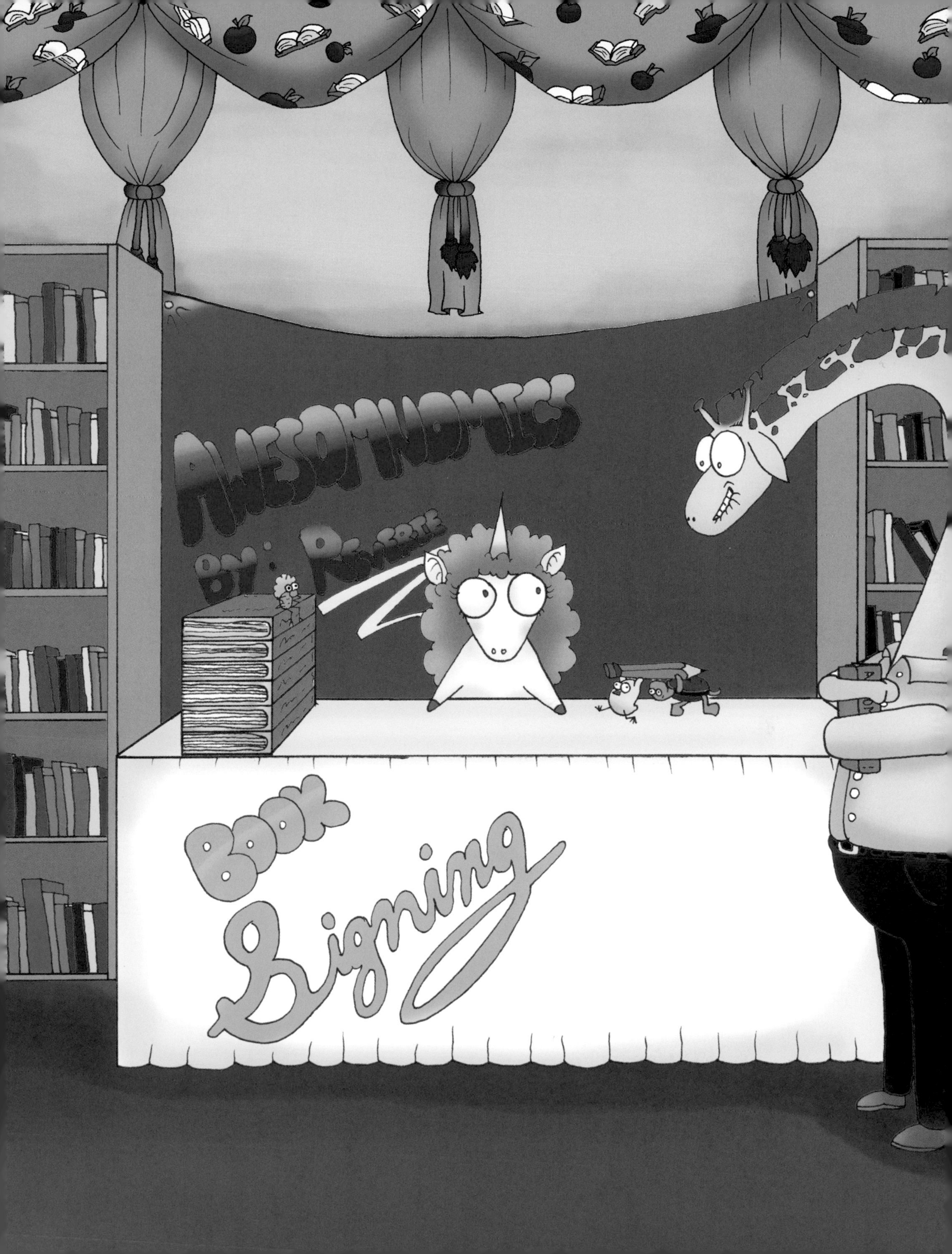
AWESOMNOMICS
BY: REVERIE
BOOK
Signing

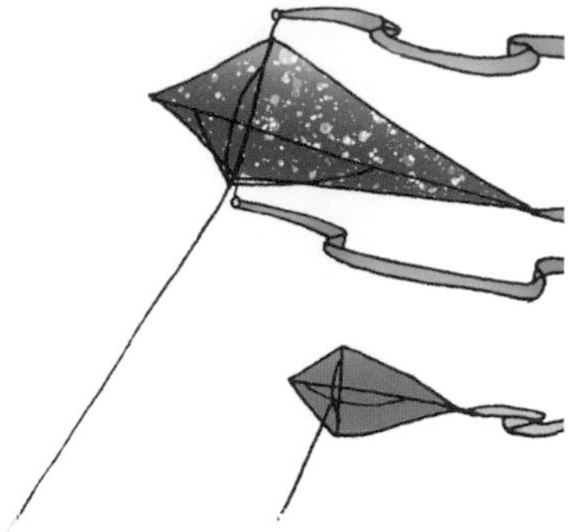

Her plant shop grew such special flowers,
They sparkled just like her...
No one could grow flowers like these,
it was hers that they prefer.

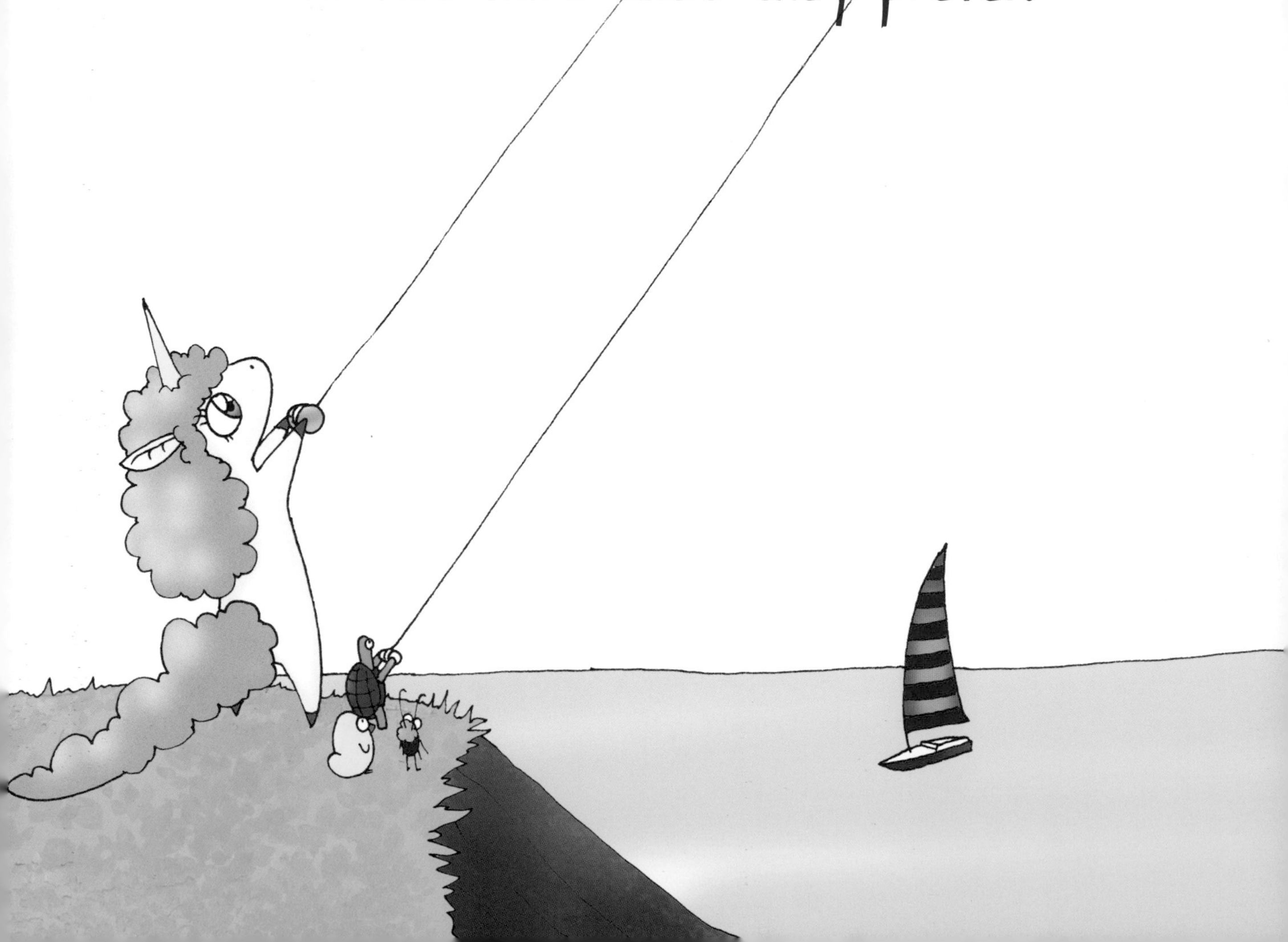

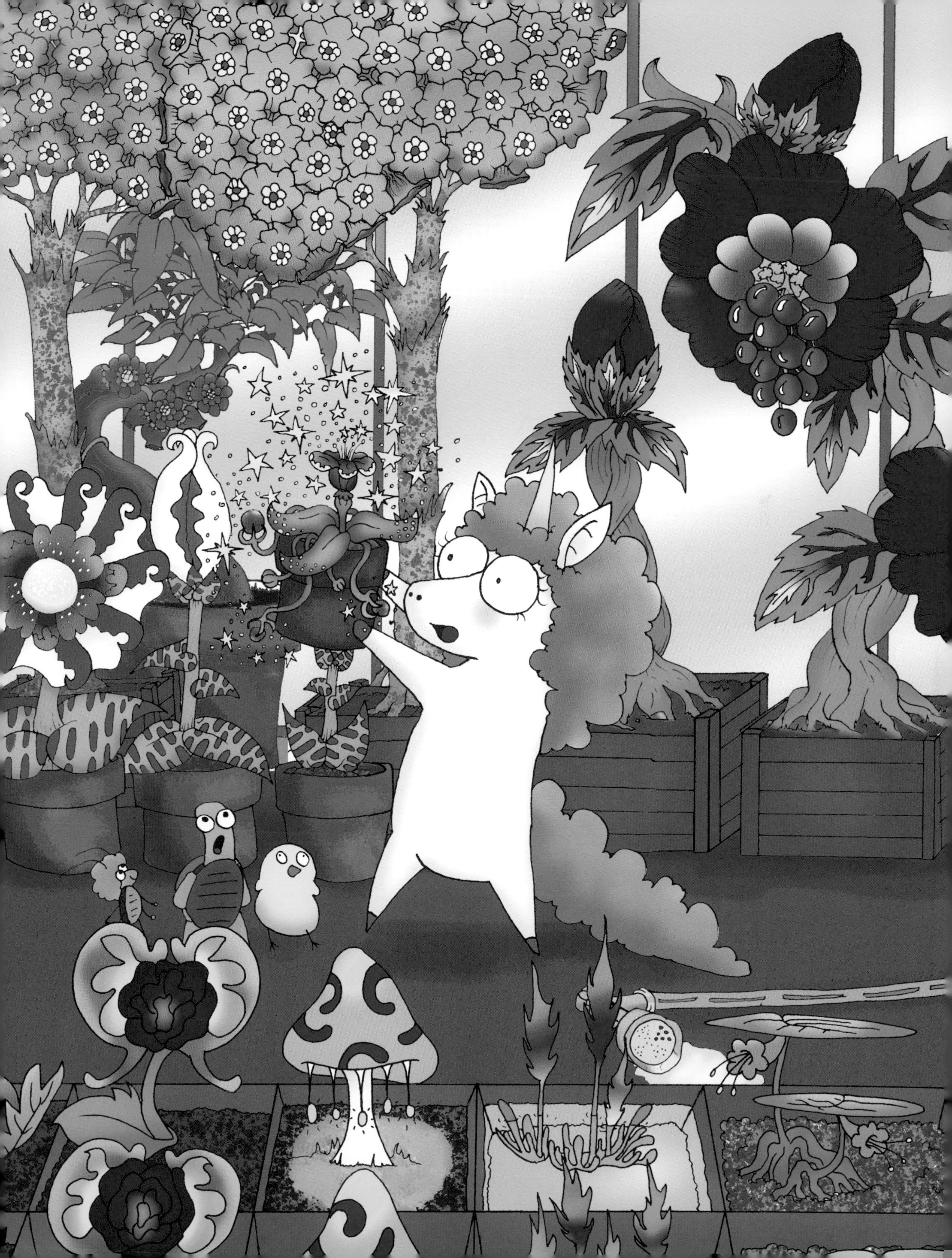

Reverie, when asked to speak,
Taught others to believe...
And with hard work and diligence,
Any dream you can achieve!

The End

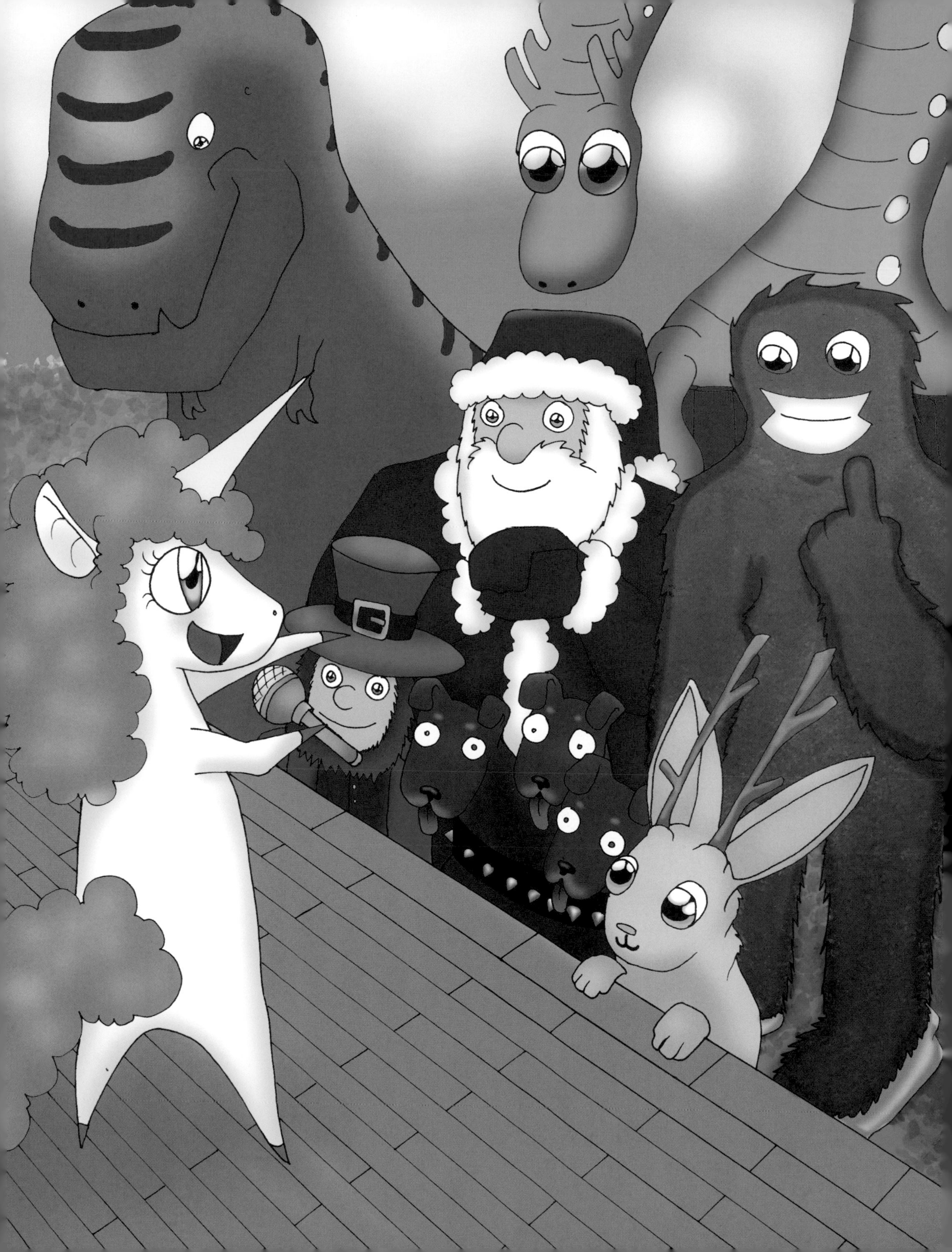

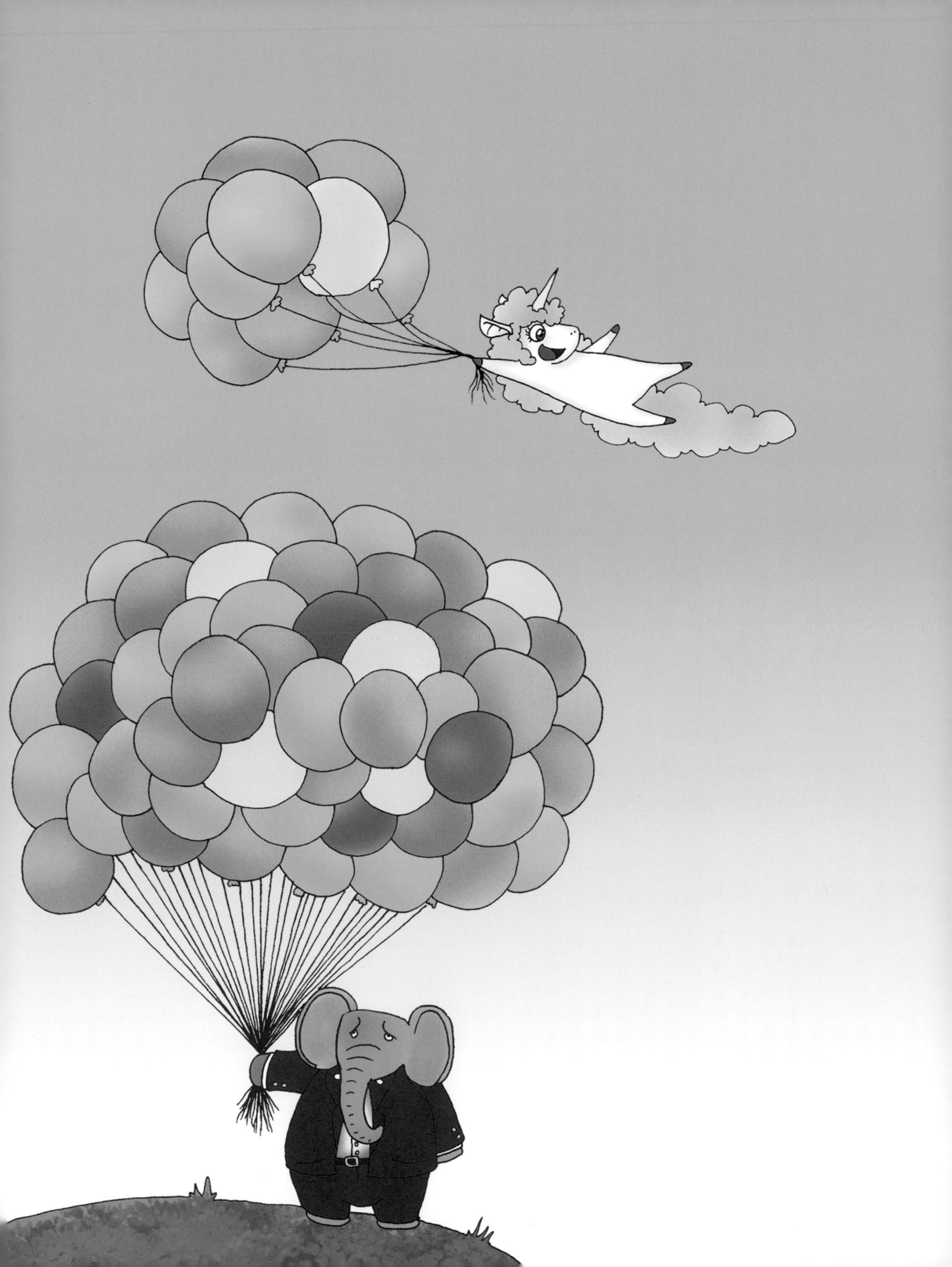

💚 Claim Your FREE Gift!

Visit ➡ PDICBooks.com/Reverie

Thank you for purchasing Reverie,
and welcome to the Puppy Dogs & Ice Cream family.

We're certain you're going to love the little gift
we've prepared for you at the website above.

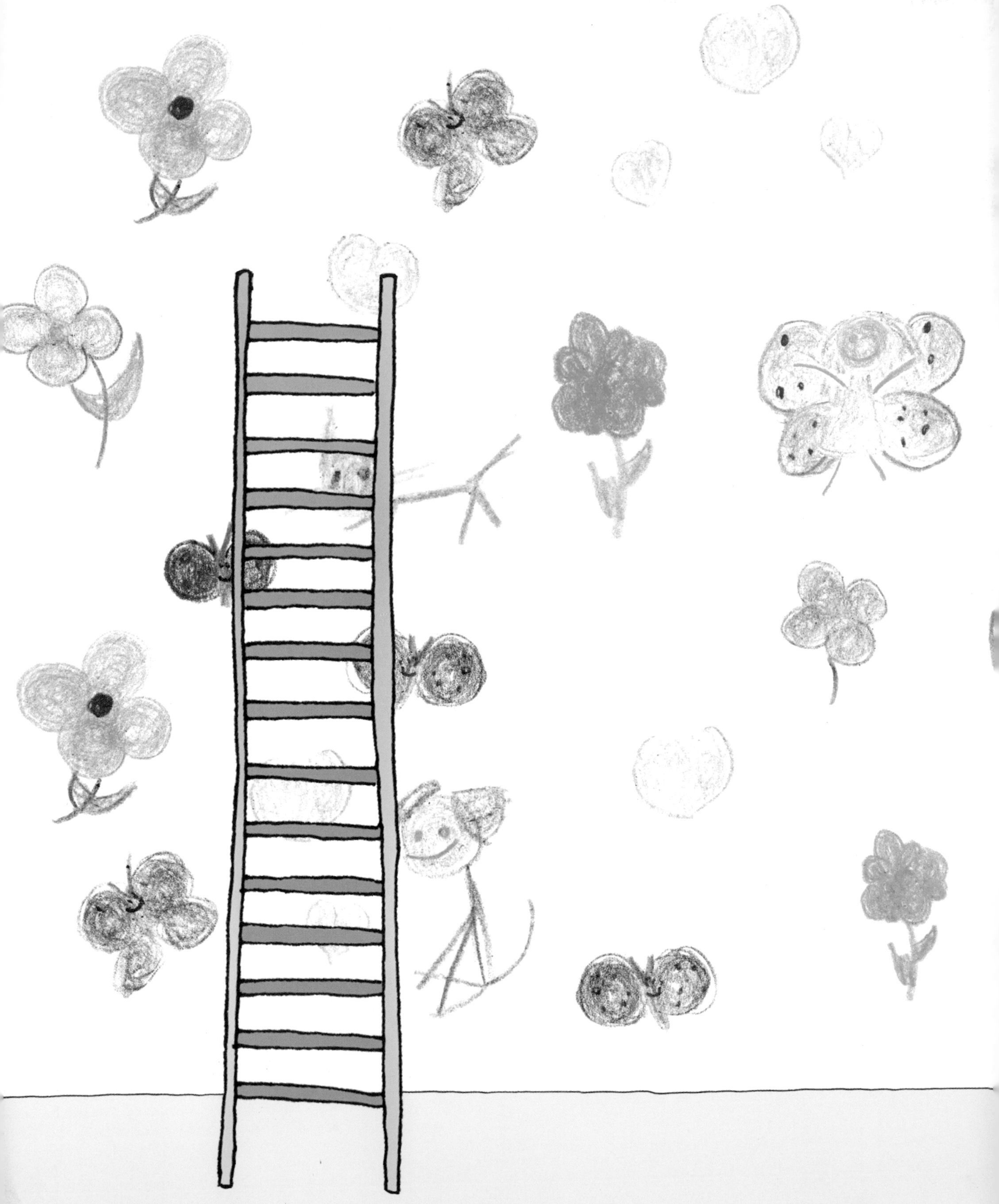